AF370473

Awoken before the evening should

A novel

Thibault Jacquot-Paratte

Cyberwit.net
HIG 45 Kaushambi Kunj, Kalindipuram
Allahabad - 211011 (U.P.) India
http://www.cyberwit.net
E-mail: info@cyberwit.net

Printed at Repro India Limited.

"Morgen schon ist hier das Schweigen,
Und vielleicht in der Luft
Noch das Rascheln von Kränzen
Und ein verwesender Duft.

Aber die Nächte werden
Leerer nun, Jahr um Jahr,
Hier, wo dein Haupt lag und leise
Immer dein Atem war."
* - Georg Heym, Letzte Wache*

"All we can do is constantly to notice when we begin to act badly, to check ourselves, to go back, to coax our weakness and inspire our strength, to call upon the names of virtues of which we know perhaps only the names. We are not good people, and the best we can hope for is to be gentle, to forgive each other and to forgive the past, to be forgiven ourselves and to accept this forgiveness, and to return again to the beautiful unexpected strangeness of the world."

-Iris Murdoch, The nice and the good

For Chris Bristol,

Better was the time for which we knew each other.

1

The train was coming in late – and much later than it should have, having been held up by the patrols that checked passports and *documents*, even as we didn't cross borders – into the city, and as clouds were low and humidity was condensing into light fog, it all seemed purplish blue, the way the streetlamps and storefronts reflected, pushed together, tightly wound, cramped in the capital. "Ivan must still be waiting at the station, expecting delay for one problem or another" thought I ("he should have; I had"), if they were to let us arrive this evening at all.

-      Sorry, are you done with your paper? I was wondering... a lady asked the tweed clad gentleman seated in front of me.

-      We're all very anxious, he stated, nodding, holding out the day's issue to her, as if nothing had been more natural than to share it.

Staring into the mauve night, I realized that here too, it must have rained. Our wagon reeked of the suffocating stench of damp clothes on tepid skin, of wet socks clamping their wearers' feet under still soaked shoes. I hadn't thought the storm had stretched all this way, as for some distance, rain had stopped beating on the wagon's windows. Perhaps it had been two storms, separate yet similar, with their own varying intensities, simultaneous, or it had been a single outburst from above, blown from this direction against our meeting, leaving here its debris. I didn't know; neither weather nor news had ever been much of interest to me, and never had I made it less of my interest as now. If rain had been to come, so should it come, and those people who had listened to bulletins, and had been conscious of threatening downpour, had stepped out and were wet as well. It was no longer raining now, and I had been let through the barricades; that was all I needed.

2

Ivan was unmistakable – recognizable from the first step I took out of the railway car. Of course, it helped that the station was almost empty; the only occupants were a dozen heavily monitored individuals (one of whom was Ivan), and uniform clad pawns (the watchers), some holding heavier weapons than others, some holding the leashes that held back the enormous man-eating mutts equally on alert – their pointy ears stiffened, snouts upwards tilted – but not the passively vigilant way dogs usually are in these places, and I had been told about this, so I was at least at ease about the dope I had in my case (the only article of luggage I had brought besides a small backpack ; in my case, next to my instrument, I had stuffed my clothes, my music, my toothbrush, and the remainder of what I would need for the few shows which, we hoped, would launch our new album – the hardest one to produce, not solely because of this paranoid social climate in which moving around, meeting, and recording, had become increasingly difficult, but because of the new distance between we band members – and hopefully, if *they* would allow it, a short launch tour). The authorities were now busying themselves so with everything regarding the average person's day-to-day, that they disregarded what they used to freak out about. *Substances* were easier to come by than ever before (granted, depending on the substance), and no one cared. The guards wished to spot spies and agitators, and in their patriotic frenzies, scoffed at our MDMA, shrooms, methamphetamines, or whatever we started taking (some of us did start taking new and different *vitamins*, as we enjoyed these more than the conflicts outside, whatever those conflicts were, what they supposed, mayhap meant or represented).

Beyond the row of guards, ordering us (and not asking) to once again show our identification documents and state our purpose in this, our capital (as some said "for the time being, at least, lest should it change"), Ivan was clearly visible, sitting on a bench, aloof (unlike the other *waiting ones*, stiff like scarecrows, fear exuding from their postures, glares, and hairs raised as if by ghastly static), as he didn't even appear to pay too much attention to the long awaited train which had just stopped at the nearby platform. He was looking upwards (to the wonderful painted ceiling no doubt – strewn with stars, blue lines drawn soft, like fibres dangling off of ripped silk cloth, in traditional motifs), exercising his fingers over an old classical guitar, which I remembered as being his first ever guitar (one of those cheap boxes one might get to learn on, but on which the action of the strings is so high, that beginners often get discouraged and spooked, barely able to play a single note – an instrument which he gladly kept not only out of nostalgia, but as it was so hard to play, that after focused practice, his current axe felt like a breeze, on which he could jam indefinitely with great ease; a bit like those athletes training with weighed equipment). He was nonchalantly dressed in an *olde suit* (he'd had it for years, and wore it when he didn't need to look too-nice; plus, he claimed that the look of an *olde suit* suited a musician, or other artists, and working people, not only because the average creator couldn't always afford the spic-and-span latest fashion, – an affirmation of status – but also because the *worn* showed that they were busy at work), and had, hanging at his collar, something between a cravat and a loose bow tie, reminiscent of romantic poets, all too tallying with today's fashion.

I wanted to wave and shout. He surely would have heard me, as deathly still as this place was (I had never seen it so empty when I was still living in this city, before I chose to move along with my girlfriend, as she had gotten a job not too far away, and a commute would still have been possible in essence – though this had proven more challenging than anticipated – and there where we now lived, I was able to do some work with K.L.U., a nice little up-and-coming singer of pop that was *okay* enough for me to be involved with, not that there were any substantial earnings associated with that work either yet, it was something to help live by). I stopped myself from making any big gestures to get any attention (not only Ivan's), as I would surely have gotten arrested for it. The military, or so the authorities had become, saw almost all civilian travel as suspicious – they barely wanted to sell me a ticket when I was making the final preparations; they said, instead, after thirty minutes of interrogations about the purpose of my short trip, that I should do like everyone, and barricade myself in, that if I would sign up for the new citizens' militia, I might still be able to qualify for training, and receive a weapon (at least some old rifle they would have confiscated from private dealers, the official had smirked). But I'd be damned if I'd get dragged into a mess that wasn't mine – not mine to begin with, not mine to be made mine. And though it was incredibly difficult at that train station counter window, with the death-dealers at every corner, Argus-eyeing me, two-handedly gripping their instruments of murder, not to tell that *man* to stuff his patriotism deep in the compost pile with other decaying waste, and I refrained from being condescending since I was aware that doing so would definitely prevent me from getting a ticket, and it should even land me in the slammer (from what I had heard, the emergency measures had become that strict), I did manage to keep a cool head, and persuade him calmly that this trip was important enough – I improvised some nice sounding statements about music being essential to peoples' morale, about not stopping normal life from going on, yada yada yada – and remind myself, that the most important was to remain as little associated with these people, their ideals, their ideas, and their orderly vision of chaos as possible. And the best way to remain unaffiliated, was to smile and nod, a plastic smile, not contradicting them, not flipping them the bird, not clearly opposing them, but remaining silent, even naif or clueless if one will; not an ally, and not a foe, just some imbecile that they shouldn't bother with. Those people couldn't conceive that who they would consider an imbecile was in fact brighter than they, and thus, it would serve no purpose to quibble. I wouldn't engage in futile activities. There is too much beauty in the world for that, too much to be occupied with; no time to tell off the brown-shirts.

Instead of calling out to my friend, my brother, I lugged my heavy case in front of me, stepping down the line to the inspections, and tried to get into my own mood, my own bubble, once more, as he, Ivan, had certainly done (he was undoubtedly in a haze of melodies and daydreams) not to die from the ambient tension. Soon enough, between the green and white pillars, the tall archways, under the bright blinding dull yellow indoor lighting, I would come up next to him, he would instantaneously snap out of his reverie, he would stand, put his hand on my shoulder, and I would lay my hand on his. He would slip his guitar into his canvas bag, I would adjust my bowler hat, and we would get out of this *checkpost* without uttering a single word that could be deformed against us.

3

I was withdrawn as they rummaged through my belongings, and emptied my light luggage into trays, even feeling up the linings, probably to see if they had been resewn, or if they were faulty at some places, though I did have butterflies in my stomach from anxiety that they would rip my case – they had already handled my bass with so little care that I had almost lost my aloofness (don't ding my bass – it's older than you are!). But this diligently preserved zen dissipated into an agitated rush when I took to the task of repacking, all the while a heavyset bald male who wore a rabid grimace and brandished a cattle prod hollered that we should speed up. Out of the corner of my eye, though I purported to it not, I caught sight of a chap who unfortunately had admired the ceiling and architecture of the edifice too lengthily, and was two fingers away from being dragged off by the guards, all the while they yelled blatant accusations into his horror-stricken visage.

Recollections of the train ride came to me. However brief a trip it should, in theory, have been, our stops at each of the numerous checkpoints, the ID controls, led our patience to rot into despair. I had distracted myself with two novels I had packed – a cheap entertaining paperback downed within a few hours, and one more substantial work that I would still take some days to finish, as some books are not meant to be read quickly, cover-to-cover, but are meant to be picked at slowly, for the reader to reflect upon the impressions left by its words. In the train's acrid atmosphere I had been reluctant to delve into such a delightful process, since concentration was scarce, and warding off migraines, challenging. Amongst the white-noise whispers of an indefinite halt, or rocked by the gentle clacking of wheels on rails, I did everything in my power to chase away the rumours that slithered, hissing, venomous fangs bared, throughout the train.

The stench of we livestock filled the cars evermore, a stench I could not get used to. At some point I took a break from half-slumber and went down to the dining car where I purchased a pint of sour ale, and at no point during the walk from my seat to the bar did the same keywords stop hitting my ears. The same keywords that polluted papers, journals, contemporary writing... the same keywords that polluted some of the songs I reluctantly backed on recordings, the same keywords mechanically parroted on the TV and the radio, and the same keywords that the local grocer would sigh about or the mailman would cry about to any unassuming passerby, for the sake of complaining.

And as I dipped my lips into my mug of ale, the barman thought it proper to poke my nerves by joining in the gossip. Something or another about the risks of travel, on top of everyday risks, and it really didn't take me a long time to shut him down, by making it clear that I had no interest in discussing issues that I wanted no part in, and which worked to the detriment of myself, and everyone else. He took it the wrong way, rubbed his nose, judging me, obviously at that second considering me a threat of some sort. Off guard, I took a chance at correcting my digression, and mumbled "nerves". He seemed to take it as a valid excuse. The only important thing is that he didn't take it unto himself to report me.

Sipping my pint, those same buzzwords floated at the brim of my ears. Impossible to rid oneself of them. Like flies they zipped around, landed here and there, and no matter if I were to swat at them, or wave them away, they would come back.

The bald grimacing capo lunged his cattle prod to chase me off as I collected my few remaining items. Avoiding to respond, to interact, to acknowledge him, I swiftly spun on my heels, bagatelles in hand, to rejoin my compadre.

4

During the walk with Ivan over to his place, we spoke surprisingly little. We who, when together, could, rare as that is even with friends, have an uninterrupted conversation, flowing of its own will, without filler small talk and hollow remarks, from the moment we greeted one another, until the time of our unwilling parting. Plainly, we didn't feel at ease to say what we pleased in these streets where ears lingered in the gutters, and hidden behind trees, junction, and facades. We smiled at each other. Only briefly exchanged pleasantries. What music I had listened to on the trip, if he had any new tunes in progress... Subjects as simple as entertainment, his outings or if he had a love life at present, would attract unwanted attention. The most he dared – he inquired about my session work, and my project with K.L.U.

During our silences, I noticed the trees were in a lovely golden dress. Even though it had rained, fairly few leaves had fallen; swaying branches densely enrobed, delighted the eyes in the now ephemeral presence of their garments. Where the fog had dissipated, the stars were visible thanks to the city's reduced lighting. The city center and the central station districts were exceptions, where elements similar to normal life persisted, yet elsewhere, only specific streets remained illuminated; many monuments, billboards, signs, and more were unlit. If at first streetlamps kept us company, permitted me to notice the many-coloured foliage, the part of town where we were headed never had been glamorous to begin with, and it was now deprived of spotlights. The half crescent of the moon offered us its halo in somber lanes, to the extent that we only bothered with a flashlight when we neared Ivan's place, to counter the increased number of potholes. Ivan led the way the whole hike, given that it was my first time at his new place (during my last sojourn having snoozed under K.'s roof). The breeze was clement; its twilight heat erased the coolness of the drizzle-day.

Walking, in silence, in the evening air, looking up at this display – the opalescent stellar flares, behind those branches the tint of which my fresh recollections restored – helped me to ignore the many eyes leering us up and down, hoping for a reason to bother us. Only twice were we asked to open our cases, their contents to inspect, our Ids adjoined. We knew better than to refuse, or be difficult about it; the fastest and easiest way to get out of any problem was by going along, and acting as if it didn't bother in the least.

Be it because we were nearing Ivan's pad ("almost there" had he declared) and we were finally relaxing, or because it was legitimately intriguing, but we did get going on one topic, when I remarked that we had never incorporated any twelve-string (shocking, given Ivan's favourite make) or baritone guitar in our music ; Ivan replied that neither had we incorporated any eight string bass (the thought of acquiring a Hagström gave me a surge of adrenaline).

–   The amount of sound between you on a twelve string, me on an eight string, and K. on whatever she would cook up, I mused.

–   An organ guitar, like Vox or MCI produced like a hundred years back, Ivan burst in excited giggling before lowering his voice and scanning the alley; or one of those simulator pedals, or we get an organ player. Feels like we just came up with the concept for a next new album.

–   We need to toast to human creativity: the only thing we're worth.

Heels came to a slow trot on the sidewalk behind us, sticking to our rhythm, tailing the few turns we took, mimicking the two brief halts we sustained with the dual purpose of me clasping my case in my other hand, and to see if these new footsteps would pause as well – and they did. And so halted our conversation, since unless these footsteps belonged to some marauder in the shadows (which was unlikely trusting to the police-state), something in what we had articulated had attracted that unwanted attention.

Increasingly, attention was bad. Some parasite had infested the notion. Even for artists such as ourselves, the goal wasn't to get people talking about us, like it used to be. Now for one wrongly placed sentence, we could be imprisoned. Imprisoned for vague notions, imaginary notions, in our imaginary societies. *Treason,* I heard was one of them – a colleague of a painter friend of mine had been imprisoned for that. Which treason? How were we supposed to betray who, and when were we supposed to have sworn some sort of non-failing zeal? At birth? A newborn, before learning speech, before being able to hold up its head, should have sworn "allegiance"? Or should children who can barely count to a hundred parrot oaths? But that's not the point, I didn't care about any of that. Nor should anyone else have. The point was that we could be condemned for these mythological crimes because of just one wrongly placed... Or if we didn't get arrested, that bad attention would get us bared from every venue, contract, publicity shot... And creating experimental works, that didn't fit in any commercial perspective (even those places that claimed to promote experimentation usually just promoted *their* vision of what experimental should be), we had a hard enough time getting exposure without that exposure ruining us. My nerves ignited ablaze for an instant in that mild evening, but through the efforts I had gotten accustomed to exerting, I blew all of it away, forgot my frustrations, and focused on the lovely nighttime scenery, and the exciting days to come.

With revelatory half-smiles outlined within the pallid glow of moonbeams, Ivan and I shelved the newly birthed topic for later.

5

As we came in, I set my stuff down next to a wall, paint peeling from its scaly, crinkled surface meandrous with shades of penumbra, and asked if I could wash my hands. Through a hand gesture, Ivan indicated the bathroom, adding vocally that he had no sink, only a bathtub. That became obvious when I opened the tap to wash my sweat sticky hands and saw the streak of dried spat-back toothpaste near the bunghole of the tub, and a dish rack full of dry dishes, next to that same chipped and aged enamel tub. I found a bar of soap rendered amber colour by the murky low-wattage buzzing bulb next to a bottle of vinegar and a blackened cloth – circular traces on the wall and a leftover acrid smell told the story of crude mold removal. Fumbling around, stray noise, was leaking in through the paper thin walls, but in a flat like this, no tenant would give a good goddamn about noise; a person would tolerate their neighbours' noise, and the neighbours would return the favour, not counting that in a place like this most lodgers would spend more time away than at home (this being a place to crash for blokes who'd work 12 hour union-sanctioned shifts, to save up money for later days, goals in mind, or for fast spending when they'd feel like a fiesta; people in these blocks lived here by choice, and for the most part, rejoiced at being given that choice; fancy living for later, the bunk house for now, the bourgeoisie has not stolen that liberty from me by imposing overpriced pressured consumption-yearning at every corner – I can live without shame by whichever standards I'm comfortable).

Yea, Ivan lived in one of those small, real crummy places, one of those that thankfully survived gentrification and the massive construction of surface-superficial-luxury condos no one could afford. Luckily he could rent one of these remaining dumps – luckily, yes, for that way he could still live alone (as opposed to sharing a room, in an apartment owned by who the fuck knows rich guy, where six other people also lived, adapting in sharing a kitchen and a bathroom without stepping on each other's toes, working out a schedule for everyone's activities, a busy environment in which he would suffer finding ways to practice), and save money to purchase the expensive gear he fancied, such as the beautiful Rickenbacker 330 he had ponied up this way. No other way could he have afforded it (keeping in mind the high cost of these scantily produced, much envied vintage machines, and that his music – when on his own, playing for others, or our band – hadn't as much success one could have hoped for... not enough to claim a respectable income in any case... and even less since *unmusic* had resurfaced).

Such a right famed instrument, yielding the jingle-jangle sound he sought (on top of the stereo rick-o-sound output, or the wonderful tonal range), also – I knew this – filled part of his ego, giving him status; a high-end instrument for a high-end serious musician, albeit he liked to claim that the price was in the sound. As for myself, I could feel scarcely a difference with many a good normal-price ranged instrument, either in tone, sound, feel, or durability (generally speaking; it all depended on which tone, feel or sound one wanted; K. argued with him about that, that he forgot some instruments had initially been considered cheap only to become envied rarities later on, because of certain particularities; with examples such as original *student model* Fender Mustangs, Duo-Sonics and Broncos). Then again, I also had my own fetishes, the culmination of which was my Orfeus Hebos bass, which I had worked so hard to find, as so few of them had been made and survive to our day and age (especially the ones stylized with the diagonal thick-lined, light-blue and cream-white, so-called *"fireworks"* or *"search light"* design on the archtop body) before these basses went out of production, when the Bulgarian public music company closed around the time they became a liberal state (unfortunately, as they well could have kept on producing these gorgeous instruments, in my opinion). He liked the expensive fineries, and I liked the vintage eccentricities, although Rickenbacker was, even in more recently produced specimen, both, vintage in sound and feel (naturally, our instruments *fit* together as they fit with our music), and it wasn't like eccentricity couldn't be fine (I wouldn't have chosen my instrument just for its look – or I could have modified it, old though it was, the specific one I had made in the late 1970's – but the low-output chromed brass encased pickups gave off pure warmth teamed with flatwound strings, such was the sound I was after, and I enjoyed the big body and overly narrow neck) though it was much harder to find a *distinctive* instrument than it was to find a *good* instrument (K. knew that better than anyone).

6

I woke up on his filthy couch before the sun was done rising. For sure, the days were getting drastically shorter. I was a bit bummed that my old pall hadn't given me more than one smelly blanket to cover myself with, and nothing to slip underneath myself – a sheet – so that I could avoid having my face up against the old, greasy, crumb covered, smelly, couch cushions, on which I had just slept; then again, sleep wasn't what I was here for, and at least it was nice to slumber in his no-frills nest. I never understood people who would refuse to house a friend because their place wasn't "nice enough" - what do you care about *nice enough* (whatever that means) if all you're after is a dry place to crash? I had never turned down a friend, and Ivan was that way, and I was happy to be staying with him at such an exciting time in our careers – so we hoped – even though the whole world didn't seem to want to let us *do well*, have success, take an interest in what we strove to accomplish. I stored the sweater I had used as a pillow in my case, and got up, took a few steps towards the minuscule kitchen (which was separated from the minuscule living room with – literally – a plywood partition, decorate with spring-flower pattern wallpaper). Ivan was preparing breakfast – cheese and vegetable omelette – and brewing our first of many coffees of the new dawn. It was bound to be a long day, and we would likely be out until the 1AM curfew we were forced to obey (at the risk of being shot), no matter how little we cared for it. We were just happy it was 1AM in this burg, and not earlier like some of the more vocal *schizos* wanted.

We had an interview on the morning radio, recorded at 8am, to be played at 9am (there could be no more live broadcasts unless they came from the *authorities* themselves, forcing stations to prerecord shows; as the interview was to be an hour long, it would take the censors that hour to listen to it, allowing it to be played an hour later, counting on no editing necessary). The interview was one reason to be up so early. We also had to practice a lot, on account of us not having been able to play together since our last recording sessions, about two months ago. We all trusted we knew our parts, and had older material which we knew by heart and were beyond comfortable with. The band members who lived in the city had practised a little; the problematic ones were myself, who needed to take the train in order to come (and according to the authorities who dealt out *inner-state travel permissions*, band practice weren't considered part of a musician's job – their reply to any objections were stubborn nonsensical statements such as "if you practice alone sufficiently, there is no need for you to practice together" or such –, though they had given them to me for recording sessions and a concert, after I provided supporting documents) and H., our drummer, who lived in the suburbs, and had almost been arrested the last time she tried to move her drum set around, as anyone transporting large items these days were thought to smuggle prohibited items). We were to practice all afternoon, inasmuch as our release show was tonight, at The Rails – which normally would have been too big to be open nowadays, but owing to it being underground, they were able to arrange for it to resume its activities, with modified safety regulations (the manager had told us this, laughing that *they* were less afraid of people blowing stuff up underground – the authorities didn't think it would do serious damage if anything disruptive should emerge from within the fortified concrete vault which was The Rails – and with daily searches, and close surveillance, it was impossible for it to serve as an arms cache. It would probably have been more dangerous for the authorities to close the joint down, under these circumstances).

I always liked The Rails, though, by no means was it the most prestigious club in town. It had advantages from which we had benefited. Back when things were normal, they were open 24/7 on the weekends, offering live entertainment throughout the twilight hours, and so they hired us often. They liked us. Since they were subterranean, it was a place to fearlessly play raw material fore audiences, and we could test our sound at high volume (high volume was encouraged, in fact, as it covered the rumbling, vibrations coming from the subway lines, which were slightly audible – thus, their name). Granted, we frequently had shifts in the range somewhere between two and six AM. Those less-choosy time frames allowed us to experiment on a lot of numbers and techniques. On the other hand, even the regulars agreed that the ventilation was bad (it was stuffy, and stank: perspiration, alcohol, smoke...), it was bothersome to climb down the stairwells leading to it from the street; their elevator for bringing down equipment was ancient, slow, and had occasionally been broken – on those occasions, all the night's bands lent and borrowed equipment, instead of hauling their individual gear up and down the endless stairs, a borderline impossible feat (what lovely trusting camaraderie, minding each other, glad to help, not rivalrous; and for the borrowers, a drill in testing unfamiliar gear and settings, performing stellar out of habit). There were other benefits, other inconveniences, but all in all, it was a splendid joint.

The Rails' history was pretty interesting. I was told it had been a large atomic shelter formerly linked to multiple apartment complexes aloft, in those days when they built bunkers a bit everywhere, in massive strikes of obsessive stubborn distrust of every other regime as ready to kill everyone off as they were (preparing, or prepared, for that most horrendous we knew ourselves capable of – much as right now, though, fuck it). Fallen into disrepair, those apartment complexes were torn down, and the office buildings, hotels, stores, and newer apartment blocks presently above The Rails were built. The thing is that this shelter was so heavy, so impressively solid, gigantic, and hopeless to take apart, that they had, at first, decided to simply bury it, and leave it to be forgotten (much like every large city retained kilometers of forsaken underground galleries). That was until the Musicians' Collective heard about it. At that time, the collective was a small organization, with only a few cooperative stages. They saw this literal "hole" as an opportunity to have, at last, a very large stage – and so they managed to purchase it cheap from the municipality. I was never too clear about how the cooperatives ran these places though, nor how the cooperative worked; I never cared about the politics of it all, much as with politics, though we were all members of the Musicians' Collective.

When Ivan served breakfast, two tall glasses of orange juice stood next to our coffee cups. "Juice and coffee? Aren't you afraid you'll fucking, have to piss all the time?", I opinionated, remembering how java went straight through his system, and he became a human fountain if his cup of Joe was downed along other beverages. Last time we toured, we occasionally asked K. to get into long guitar solos, centre-stage, so that he could sneak off to take a leak. The rest of the band, we ended up asking him if he wanted us to know more songs with just one guitar part, to give him strategic or extended breaks, to which he responded "And let K. play rhythm? She's no rhythm guitarist!", instigating another clash between the two players; we settled it by switching their parts on one tune, showing that K. could effortlessly handle the duties associated with rhythm guitar, and Ivan had no challenge taking lead (then the tour ended, so did their sibling-like spats, and we all took a break from coffee). After running his fingers through his ashen hair and straightening his horseshoe moustache with an index and thumb, he shrugged "Yea but... juice is great, man". We laughed at the same time the street visible through the window turned yellow, tinted by first rays to reach it, and we laughed, for, as mysterious as humour, friendship, and feelings work, we remembered at once the numerous reasons why we shared this strong, full-understanding friendship.

7

Though the streets weren't yet very crowded at this early hour (the city itself had never had such a low population – many had evacuated to the countryside if they could, or had left the country altogether, that was, until other nations started denying entry to our citizens; one of the reasons why we hadn't been able to get any of the visas we henceforth needed in order to be able to tour). The remaining citizens worked from home, if possible, or relied entirely on public transit, and avoided walking, as it was thought to have become dangerous despite the radical security measures (what a bunch of morons).

It was brass monkeys at dawn (damned if I knew why after the tepid midnight breeze), though I savoured the brisk invigorating qualities of this, in my mind, wonderful morning, a morning for us to deliver our sonic medicine, and resurrect the forsaken – through neglect moribund become – ill of our barbarous society. We would promote our album, release the album, play music, be in contact with others like us who had not lost their minds to fear. Music would resolve the sum of bad feelings – each and every day, my problems resolved upon hearing my instrument's low thump, and its voice would in turn resolve the problems of others. The silence of this metropolitan morning awoke in my mind the melodies we had composed – our songs sounded in my ears along with Ivan's gab (for arose fewer suspicions during the daytime; we now chit-chatted freely, carelessly deliberating, laughing, thinking out loud).

It was with much astonishment that we walked straight into a well remembered figure (an annoying one). He was an old acquaintance – a friend of a friend, and never more than that, never transmuted into a friend of one's own. He was the loathed brainy type, who made you feel bad for not being the brainy type, who wore brand-name sneakers, enjoyed shaving, getting a haircut regularly, and flaunting his cash. My friend – the one through whom I knew this dude – he was the type of intellectual who had had the same worn-out leather jacket (bought used) for the last 15 years, and could talk about the economy and beer – the two separate subjects juggled – in the same "naked", unpretentious, *unpretended*, conversation. That brain-type I liked, because even though he had a tendency to explain things I didn't want explained, and hold long speeches about subjects I desperately wanted to avoid (the bullshit economy most of all), he nodded and decreed "okay" if we told him that we really didn't give a damn. Only once I saw him get angry at someone, because they said they didn't want to vote. Other than that, he was fine. He was a childhood friend of Mila, who, she, was a good friend of mine.

The acquaintance was smoking in the street, his hands slightly trembling, his body, thin, under a black silk suit.

-    How've you been faring, inquired this acquaintance whose hair had greyed as considerably as his skin since the last time I hadn't been able to avoid his pretentious presence.

-    Pretty good! Pretty... well! I replied; we're releasing our album today. You should buy a ticket, join the crowd, at The Rails tonight.

-    Is this really a time to be going out? He frowned aggressively rhetorical.

-    As good as any!

-    Right, mh-hm, as good as any. Ha. You aren't... he hesitated, knocking the ash off his cigarette; you aren't afraid? Concerned?

-    I don't get concerned about what I don't want concerning me.

-    Have you ever had trouble taking a shit, asked Ivan.

-    What? He queried.

- You look a bit stiff, a bit stuffed up. I hear there are more constipated people than we're led to believe. Been eating a lot of white rice, a lot of meat, too few vegetables?

- What sort of question is that in a time like this. The stores are half-empty, import and export are down to nothing, and you ask me if... if...

- If you're having any trouble shitting, confirmed Ivan, before adding; well, think of adding some fiber to your diet. Never a bad time to think about your heath.

And we went our way.

We withheld our laughter for a block, and then to Ivan I mused that I forgot why I ever went out without him. He replied "because marriage is an outdated concept".

8

However few the locals were to be spotted, each and every one of them shared a harrying air of profound boredom. Their sagging mouths, vacuous and watery eyes, slumped backs, dangling arms, and slow, vague movements. That's not entirely true – a select few were tense and twitchy – had their necks sunken into their upraised shoulders, and hung their heads low, as if to avoid something (getting hit by a low flying bird?), and checked obsessively over their humps. They were blasé out of their painful distorted bodies. They scoured for anything to be excited by, for a reason to feel their hearts pounce, accelerate, for life to snap out of stagnant putrefaction. Those who remained able to walk outdoors had given up on entertainment, and unshackled their taut animuses – freely scavenging, devouring garbage. They no longer stalked intellectual sustenance, and their fantasies had stopped sighting masked assailants in the shadows, and expecting air-raids when their refrigerators started humming. These sad saps needed to go to a bar, get a drink, see a movie, argue loudly about what they had seen, leaf through pages of large-print in bookshops or libraries, or go to concerts that would awaken their souls, set them ablaze, revive the now deceased yearning they possessed (if yearning they had ever possessed; it's probable that a fraction of them had been as bored before this season of inflicted dread, as some people never felt intense sensations, never had goals, never found a reason to be happy – they lived yet).

They bewildered me – this morning was so lovely.

9

To get into the radio station, we had to be shaken down from head to toe – as if walking the mostly desolate streets, under the disapproving gaze of watchmen (professional and volunteer) – hadn't been displeasing enough. We had walked to the station with Ivan, 45 minutes by foot though it was, including the checkpoints, since it would have been so tediously complicated to take any form of the remaining public transit. Before this whole crisis, it would have taken perhaps 20-25 minutes, but now, there were so many protocols whatever we did. Here at the radio station, people were waiting for us, security knew who we were; nonetheless, we had to follow procedures that had been put in place. At the door, they were once again opening our cases, and were even suspicious about the fact we had hollow instruments (could something be hidden inside, they barked). To think the guards weren't music lovers, we had to explain that they were pretty standard instruments – that there was nothing *strange* about hollow-body instruments.

At last let in. K. and Sim were already there alongside Maria, our friend who worked at this station. Sim nervously waved, hand raised above his shiny shaved head for a brief second; K. tall and slim simply stood wearing her enigmatic smile of a thousand charms, and Maria bobbed her head left to right, eyebrows raised along her broad grin, enough for the bindi on her forehead to wobble. She had arranged that this morning there should be a whole hour retrospective about our "artistic journey". We were prepared to talk about this album, our three past albums, and our tours. After a round of hugs, Maria led us through the halls, directly to the studio where our interview would be recorded, to be hopefully played only with an hour's delay, if the listening censors would allow – the station still tried its best to maintain the same ambiance as a live broadcast would have had; the host and Maria teased that unless something were to go horribly wrong, there would be no retakes, and that songs were the only breaks; the recording would be done in one shot. Maria told us how happy she was, that she hoped this would be our breakthrough, that she loved our music, and that the populace should rejoice about hearing some good news (however marginal the news of a new album was). K. probed "No good news?", and Maria replied "Are you kidding? There was firing last night around the border. Worse..." To turn away from that convo, I asked Sim if he knew when H. was planning to show up. Sim offered an exasperated look and sighed "The road blocks on the outskirts of the city. They're searching her van; she called to say she would be late."

- Fucking Christ, can't a gall drive her van into town anymore? They've got tanks, what are they afraid of a van for?

- Weapons: grenades, assault riffles, sabotage instruments... I suppose? mumbled Sim, in a nonchalant way, making sure he wasn't being overheard.

- Well dammit, who in the city are they so scared will get their hands on weapons? Come on!

- You don't read too much, do you? Offered Sim, before adding ; I don't either, so I can't answer, but I've heard supposed tons of people out there are mutinous.

- Let them have their mutiny without us, I blurted when Maria interrupted us.

"Ready? We'll start in 10 minutes, so if anyone has to go to the bathroom, or would like a drink... You'll have breaks, but still, no drinks in the studio". We all turned to Ivan who declared "I'm good" – he had just returned from the john.

10

After 30 minutes, I stepped out during a song, to take a break from the interview. I was out in a sort of lounge, listening to the others over a speaker set up for said purpose – the host was kidding around "looks like the bass player left us for now. Aren't those guys supposed to be discrete anyway?" I had brewed myself a cup of tea when I spotted H.'s face coming around the corner.

We greeted each other in the usual fashion – a big hug. She told me she had forgotten how this place was, and I asked her if it wasn't too horrible getting here. She said "you know, of all the things, at least there's no traffic. I enjoy there being no traffic jams, I always hated those. You know, in the day, I used to get a nice latte and a piece of cake and read after every practice, because I had to do something and wait for rush hour to be over. If I'd've left straight away, I'd've sat in traffic for three hours. With the price of gas, and the environmental mayhem, might as well have coffee and cake. After enjoying those, reading a bit, I could avoid getting stuck." I told her "I think you told me, or maybe it was K.?" She replied "Yea, maybe, she used to sit with me sometimes. We'd talk a bit, or she'd read too. She always read the weirdest things though". I asked her "Books about electrical engineering?" She said "Yea, no, yes she reads those, but I was thinking about weird novels, or these thick volumes of poetry. Like 600 or 800 pages of poetry. She's the only person I've ever seen read page-by-page a book of poetry, or read a poet's complete works cover to cover. And she'd take breaks. Tilt her head upwards, read a poem again. I could see she was really thinking, right?" I concluded "Yea well, K. is something else. But we all do that a little, at least, when we read more consequential works, that we should think about, or shouldn't read fast".

I showed her to the studio, and came in between two songs, to be warmly greeted. The songs playing were from our second album. What a flashback! I seldom listened back to it. Ivan and Sim later stated that they did, underlining the importance of returning to one's previous work. If not to contemplate hit-and-misses, what aged well, what is timeless, then just to remember our sound – not to stay put, but not to stray too far away from what we were, who we are known to be. I've heard it said by other artists too, that one has to return to one's earlier works to remind oneself that one's work isn't total shit. It's frankly quite easy to despise your previous work, when you keep on moving ahead, trying to be better, or make something more interesting – acquiring different knowledge, or becoming over-critical (and we all know that having to defend our work against critics, opinions, thousands of questions pouring in from all sides, that we become overly critical). And some exhausted artists don't manage to return to their earlier works, unable to bear a glance at yore or yonder.

It had been great fun recording that album, was what I remembered. A lot of people thought we were crazy because we wanted to record the album on magnetic tape first – not digital. An insane notion given that magnetic tape bands were hardly produced anymore, and the stocks which were, were expensive and difficult to acquire. And the machines with which we could record on magnetic tapes were preciously protected by their owners. A few understood though, that tape picks up some stuff that digital doesn't. Sim was in his really occult phase, and was certain that we would pick up a ghost (or ghosts) on the tape. "Digital doesn't pick up the paranormal! It has to be physical! They can alter physical things! This is physical! They've been following me... I know it, they have, I've messed with voodoo, done too many spells, I've contacted them too many times. That's why my toaster caught fire, why my shoelaces keep on breaking, and why Ivan keeps on getting nose bleeds. But it's worth it, you know, that they are here, that they hang around me. We will have them on our tapes. We will hear them – people will hear the undead on our album". That's why we only hesitated on the LP titles "Undead album" or "Unlive album" (this one, we picked in the end), though K. liked the title *Frankenmusic* (she was the only one who liked it). The DJ played one of the songs on which Sim argued a spirit could be heard. He couldn't make out what the spirit would have been saying – that might be because, from what I recall, it was me scratching the length of my strings between the tailpiece and the bridge at that point who made that sound – Sim claims we can hear bass notes, so that it would be impossible, though I think what we hear are just hammer-ons and pull-offs. In any case, it was fun hearing a track from that album again, as again, in general I too rarely go back and listen to our recorded work, and I almost forget that what we play is really good. I'm just caught up in the fun and dynamic of doing what we do.

I had walked out again after arguing on air with Sim about if we did or didn't hear spirits. In reality, and more than that, I had nothing to say, or rather, I didn't want to have anything to say, so while the others were busy rambling into the large chrome plated microphones, I poked around this old studio I hadn't seen in a long while. The thick cushion noise-absorbing padded walls, the furniture of time darkened wood, the window offering a view upon one of my favourite squares in the city (at the centre was a large granite sculpture representing a human, turning to liquid, merging with a moon-like sphere; the explanation was astronomy, hanging over our fortunes as it regulates the tides – did the artist know how up-to-date it would be now, about 70 years after it was unveiled?), and around its pedestal, beds of flowers neatly arranged around short bushes of fragrant boxwood (on benches, around the square, enjoying the somewhat calm moments of this neurotic day, women on work-breaks; few appreciating the clear weathers, yet most, most likely, unable to stand being locked intramural any longer, and were willing to "risk" the dangers of the too-too realist outdoors – no safer in reality than their offices, but more threatening, because open spaces remind us that borders, and conflicts, and patrols, and checkpoints, and armies, are a bunch bullshit that we invented and that we can dismantle, though I could never speak this out loud at the risk of god-knows-the-fuck-what, and dammit, stop thinking, fuck all of it –, walking in their burgundy, dark-green, turquoise or black corseted dresses, each adorned with comfortable slim petticoats, except for one who went without a petticoat, and another who was wearing pants and a suit jacket, and some men in similar states dressed in the usual fashion, except for two who were sporting elegant new frock coats – the type I knew Sim would wear on stage, though his surely were bound be flashier in colours than those gentlemen's brown and muddy mustard yellow ones).

11

It was after the interview as we were all drinking a cup of tea with Maria, that H. told us a bit of bitter fresh news. As it turned out, a friend who had arranged for us to have a spot where we could practice had called her that very morning. Out of their control, the district where the practice place was, had been shut off. No one knew why; no one ever explained why anything happened these days. All the friend knew, was that the streets were blocked, and no one could get in. As we all knew, it was no use bargaining; we had no choice but to go along with whatever we were told. Isn't it a strange juncture, where you have no choice but to simply do whatever another person tells you? Or let me reiterate: deal with the context established beyond your can? Obey the authority which they have, or have granted themselves – even if you don't know why they should have it. Even if nobody thinks they should have it. In this case, we all just had to do what those people in khaki uniforms told us.

"But" the news had a second part; H. revealed her friend knew of another place, downtown, in a conveniently central building. The hangout wouldn't be as private; our music would seep through the walls; people could possibly come in and bother us. It was ironic, that though guards were asserting order on every street corner, that the closing of many businesses, and the vacancy of structures, had created a succession of hidden rooms and empty passages behind facades, or so H. alleged. H. seemed to think more was going on than anyone knew, and I jeered at her that everyone certainly knew less than what was actually going on. K. asked "what do you mean?", to which I gnarled "who the fuck actually knows what's going on?", and that made everyone laugh.

Ivan tallied with a jaunty "listen, if you got us a place, you got us a place, that's all that matters!". H. muttered "Bummer we can't practice at The Rails", and K. tried Maria "No empty studio where we could practice here?" Maria tensed up, she whispered that they didn't have the right to use any studio other than the one where we had been interviewed. Access to only one studio for everything limited the possibilities of unwarranted recordings. No long-term pre-recordings – ready days ahead – were permitted, as everything to play on air had to be surveyed, even music streaming. With one studio in-and-out, content delayed only by long-enough to be listened in, there was no margin for broadcasts that would have been disapproved of... Maria counted their station lucky to still be in operation, as it would have been quick to be shut down, and for their frequencies to be overtaken by white noise. Scrambles. Scrambled thoughts. White noise of oppression. "They want to know everything that's being said, when, and who says it", she explained, and K. joshed "I guess you've never had so many listeners, eh?".

I had no interest whatsoever in what they were saying, and I allowed my mind to wander, wondering if I should change my strings. The strings I had on now were flat-wounds – not as thick as I would have wanted, but I couldn't put larger strings on my Hebros, unless I would have changed the nut (and I would have felt bad about that, given that it was the original, and in very good shape, and as the strings sat on the zero fret, I didn't need it to be in absolute perfect shape) – yet, I was considering changing to half-rounds since lately I had a hankering for more aggressive playing, and half-rounds let me do a bit of scratching (always good fun). That was, despite K. urging me to switch back to round-wounds (one of our few creative differences) – which I hadn't touched since discovering different types of strings, when I was a beginner. I would nag "why don't you play with pure steel then?" She would smirk at me. She knew that I agreed pure nickel worked best for her. And yet, she had this way of revealing nothing from what she really though. At some point I played with half-rounds, but switched when playing for K.L.U., since her pop had a Motown vibe to it (or I had decided it should have a Motown vibe, since that was what made her music worthwhile), and in consequent, a very *woody* low-down bass sound was apropos. Short-scale and hollow-body, my instrument had that ideal tone, especially when paired with flatwounds (and the single coil voice was reminiscent of original telecaster p-basses). On the other hand, changing strings would be a little strange now, considering I had had the flat-wounds when recording on this album, and the tracks were very mellow – not as voluntarily *shrill* as some of our previous stuff. This album was our dreamscape. I was hoping it would overpower the present situation in the world: help people escape, get into their own heads, laugh at it all, forget about it all, say "it's not worth it". As far as I was concerned, as little as I forced myself to be up to date with trends or tides, this was all I knew: it wasn't worth it. Our music was worth it. Books that inspired people to have a drink and enjoy a good meal, that was worth it. Sports where no one kept score, and no one felt competitive towards "opponents", only with themselves, that was worth it.

I had entirely stopped paying attention to what the others were saying, and I noticed Ivan had as well. We had the same mindset. So much so, that I had a feeling his mind had strayed onto paths similar to mine. I stepped up to see him, and he didn't notice me at first, fixated on pulling his teabag out of the water and plunging it back in, repetitively, amidst being lost in thought.

- Something about the Rickenbacker, I speculated.

- I was wondering if I should get a fretless guitar, he admitted instantly, snapping out of his daze at the sound of my voice; I know we... yesterday, twelve string or baritone, but...

- Oh?

- I know it looks redundant for a rhythm guitar player. It should be K's territory. But she thinks fretless has too little sustain. Anyways, I've been considering it for a while. Something in me feels like I'll never be a really good guitar player unless I learn to play fretless. You know what I mean?

-     I do, avouched I before taking a sip of chai; I felt that way too. I mean, I'm not that comfortable with it, and it makes me feel bad. I should be able to play a standup bass, but instead, I just dabble. Like if I'd be playing country, except I should be able to play jazz on a thing like that.

-     I know, and... fuck, I know we're not out right jazz musicians, that we just mix in what we need... and then even if when we aren't jazzy at all... often... but... then again... you're right, a standup bass. Fuck, you know, there is no reason why a rhythm guitar player shouldn't be able to play fretless. It just makes sense! Bass players play rhythm and fretless!

-     You should do it if you feel it's right!

-     Yea...

-     So... I know when you're like this it's because you have one of those pretty long-necked things on your mind. Out with it.

He smiled shyly – that smile he only had when admitting his crushes, either on girls or instruments, and in this case, him loving his 330 so much, he must have felt any attraction to another *one* adulterous, dastardly, indecent. Polyamory was for people, not instruments. We were very faithful guys, him and I; for every new bass I had gotten, I had gone through the same feelings, heartache, and now and then, I felt a bit of guilt for not playing with my other basses as often as the Hebros (I used my 68 Eko 1150 bass on one song, for the pleasure of it, since that song had a bass solo, and in the four switches the bass had, we could turn both pickups on individually, or turn them on in series, giving suddenly higher output; perfect for a solo boost, emerging from an otherwise subtle bass line. The Eko 1150 always made me think that I would have enjoyed at some point owning a bass with a rhythm\lead circuit, like some guitars had; like the series switch on my 68 Eko, added a world of possibilities when playing live... that is, for bassists like me who looked into playing more than tic-tac accompaniment).

After a moment he added "I saw an Eastwood PB fretless for sale at a good price. Not that I can really afford a good price."

-     Afford? Who cares. If the world turns to shit, which it might, even the money stashed in our pillows won't by food.

-     Yea, but, if it keeps on turning smoothly, I was supposed to go out to the mountains for my sister's wedding. You know I was going to go by blimp. If I buy the PB not only will I have to take the god damned bus, but I'll have to borrow money to do it. The bus takes forever... and...

-     Why not borrow H.'s van?

-     You think H. would loan her van for me to drive across the country? He grinned ironically.

-     Or... any other car... I mumbled; so, a blimp... long time since I was in one. Why can't we ever get a job as one of those bands that play in luxury blimps?

-     Because we don't play ballroom ballads.

-     Hm... well, if this album doesn't pan out, we should do *electric Strauss*.

-     There's an idea. You know, I'm afraid the album won't pan out. And even if it does pan out, the world won't.

-     Then, well... we've lived okay so far.

-     Speak for yourself, your girlfriend has a full-time job. I'm tired of *whoreing* myself out as a session Joe Blow to eat rice with ketchup at the end of the day.

-     That's just because you buy expensive gear. You could eat a few more veggies if you wanted to.

-     No, I've been saving up because of this wedding.

-    And now instead you want to buy expensive gear, I winked at him.

He dipped his moustache into his tea. We turned our heads, figuring we should have been heedful to what the others were doing.

12

At H.'s van, one of the security guards escorting us eyed me as though hesitating if he should once more rummage through my belongings. His glare went from my dumb-smiling countenance, to my case, to my profile anew, to the van... And yet, his pack of weapon-clad thugs had not spaced the tip of their heavy boot-toes from our heels since we had moved to depart from the radio station. Menacing entourage for sure, they were supposed to assure us we would not have to be inspected a hundredth time. Considerate of them, I'll admit! And we had patiently waited, silent in their company, while the crews of the convoy (our to-be escort) finished leaving no stone unturned in the van, and examining the undercoating. Only at the convoy-commandos' thumbs up could we approach our dear stagecoach.

Patient we were, for we had been assured this would be easier for us as well. The location we were headed to next – arranged by H.'s friend in the hot morning mix-up when we had been barred from our previous practice spot – was situated in what was deemed a *secure perimeter.* These perimeters were enclosed by military blockades, potentially subversive elements flushed out. Therefore, surveillance measures within these perimeters were as slacker as entry was restrained. How did we become part of the elite few admitted to the precinct? By which negotiations? Who gave a good god-damn, as long as the deal was signed and in our favour.

How it was explained to us, was that vehicle inspections were not done at the blockades, in the event that the vehicles should be trapped bla, bla, bla. They were done remotely, and then the a-okayed autos were escorted to be let through (as long as we did not stop at any point during this drive). Should we refuse this, the van would remain outside the perimeter, we'd have to walk through the checkpoints, get cavity probed, and lose over half the day.

The wait had a painful side to it, since we refrained from talk, from laughter (everything was suspicious for the paranoid brigades); we didn't smoke, didn't dare stir. The image of an individual waiting, holding an old-style multi-purpose phone, hopped into my mind. When I was a kid, folks had that reflex, in every dead moment, to pull out their touchscreen devices and fuddle-duddle on them. That was before the great boycott, when I was in my preteen years and we all were fed up with so-called *social* media of various sorts, of being spied on by anyone and everyone (with perpetual net connections and out-in-the open microphone phone-taps), for the sake of low-brow destructive entertainment. I recalled how absurd the situation was – one minute you were talking with your friend about some object you had heard of for the first time; the next instant, that very same object popped up in adds everywhere around you. People accepted they were spied on left and right, and were made to believe that it was accommodating, to their advantage.

In my preteens, none of us understood how it was more convenient to incessantly text-message, instead of having a quick phone call. And how the generation before us sacrificed the to-tame present of the incidental, the arbitrary, the unknown – on and off course drifting – basis of our free will and druthers, by not relinquishing their (and their access to) foreknowledge in any situation. Grown fearsome of interactions not predetermined by online matching; afraid to pick up a phone for an unnameable caller, or without looking at whether or not they should be familiar with the caller; not watching a movie without scanning a summary, or watching a trailer (but just watching the flick, because of curiosity, for the heck of watching a movie one knows nothing about); wandering city streets without a map, without a purpose, driving without a satellite view, taking directions from a printed map and road signs, or best yet, guessing the way. While the generation before us had strained themselves to create self-driving vehicles, we asked "what for? Why? Should such an idea make sense for a train or a subway, yes, but the vehicle of a sovereign individual... why?" People relinquished their ability to interact with their surroundings – actions dictated by automatic presets – and therefore, their own autonomy. Was it their dream to sit idly while everything around them self-managed? What dream was this inertia? When I grew up, we wanted a future where each individual should govern their own actions, and not be governed by mechanisms robotic.

And we emancipated ourselves; we boycotted those connective-media sites, and we boycotted those tablet-phones. What a wonderful period. We met in the physical plane, participating in all sorts of events; put our energy towards thriving... And yet... And yet now we were in such a situation, with buzz-cut maniacs eager to die and murder. Had those types also, as I had, in my high school days, sat in recycle-circles, where we dissected electronic devices we wanted repurposed? Had they also marched in "awaken-togethers" holding banners stamped with quotes from the likes of Aldous Huxley, the motto "No more Soma!", David Foster Wallace and his Infinite Jest, from Tristan Tzara and his manifestos? Had they, or had they somewhere inherited the *obedient* mindset of the generation before us?

When the *relegionnaires* had bolted H's doors back on, and put her seats back in, they signalled we could place our belongings inside. The vandal infantry didn't have the courtesy to place the items removed from the van in their place – H. gathered her bric-a-brac, and we loaded the amps, mikes, wires, again.

13

H. couldn't drive slow, and she had to drive in the middle of the road, armoured jeeps on each side of us. When the engine had started, Ivan had joked "Think they might have bugged the inside?" Though, it shut our traps, it certainly stopped any of us from uttering criticism which might have landed in oversensitive ears. So we sat in silence. Sim used his single-purpose phone to call K. who had opted to run to her atelier instead of coming with the rest of us, in order to grab the equipment she wanted, and hadn't dragged to the radio station. She would have to pass the barricades on foot; complicated, but... hey, her choice. People who do no wrong should never have to worry. Well... shouldn't.

Sim hung up, scratched at the large tiger tattoo on his bicep. A tiger, a blue sun, on upwards curved desert ground. With Ivan, we had tried to convince him to get another tattoo on his forearm – either an anchor with a random boat name, or a heart tattoo with "mom" across it. Old gags that never stop being funny. The idea came to us on the only occasion we ever played in the tropics, while we were drunk, at some shack-bar on the seaside. We annoyed him, demanding which name he'd pick for a boat if he had one. Flinging his lanky self about the cantina he insisted "I don't know, I don't know", though a spark in his deep blue eyes promised he was lying. He never told us what it would be, insisting "fuck off" instead. Since that was what he gave us as an answer, we concluded his boat was the Fuck-off. He was captain of the Fuck-off, or for short, Captain Fuck-off. When he asked us to stop calling him that, we'd ask him what else he'd call his boat; lacking an answer, we awaited his forearm tattoo, the anchor of the Fuck-Off. Or the "mom" heart tattoo. "Aye aye captain Fuck-off!"

Sim was too honest of a dude to just lie and be done with it. He hung out with we trashy people, but he was the most well-mannered among us. As a kid, he had been in choirs, had solfeggio lessons, all that jive. Deep in the cackles of his corrupted heart, he had a white, posh and a smidgen conservative background which he strove to hide, lose and obscure, not always successfully. Maybe all his tattoos were part of this attempt, or maybe they really did mean something to him. That was his excuse for not wanting the anchor-and-or-heart-mom tattoo: that they didn't come from his own self, his inner revelations, they didn't hold deeper meaning for him. Though the only meaning he had ever disclosed to us was that of a large ghost tattoo on his left calf; "leave some of your ghosts behind with every step you take" (I had joked to Ivan, yet not to Sim, that if leaving ghosts behind was the objective, what I saw, was that some clung to his heels. Albeit, maybe he was conscious of this).

Sidewalks and the fronts of buildings rushed by, blurry, H.'s foot heavy on the accelerator. I was antsy to start practicing, though it was comfortable being in the car, and riding. I closed my eyes and breathed calmly. It was a nice ride.

14

The place to which we had access was indeed right in the city centre, in one of those wonderful skyscrapers that, by now, evacuated, were virtually empty. H.'s friend had worked in the building, or something, and had the keys to the floor where she had been in charge, since it had all been shut down, and she was in charge of nothing now. Having vacated the premises did not, nonetheless, remove the fact that the company she worked for had legal access... Something, something, I didn't ask the details because the result was that we were able to come into a huge deserted hall in a recently cleared building. She reassured us that as the tower stood in the secure perimeter, the military personnel was unlikely to check up on us anew, but that it wasn't impossible that a squatter should barge in (assuming unassuming squatters had remained hidden in the secure perimeter), yet, other than that, no one was likely to inspect or use the building for a while. It was more likely to fall into disrepair or be blown up before.

A shame that this work of architecture was left to desuetude. The immensely high ceiling, art deco style, windows rounded at the top, spanning a whole wall. We brought our gear up – I plugged in first, into the amp Sim had hauled for me (he had acquired one of the same model I used; borrowing it was ideal as bringing my own, on the train, came across as incredibly gruelling). Checking my tuning, the empty, open space gave off some amazing reverb and terrible echo, but no buzz came from the glass. Impressive, as to the size of those panes.

-       Those are some pretty heavy-duty windows, Ivan pointed out.

But it wasn't long after that, that we heard like a crowd yelling: loud, aggressive ruckus. The others were still setting up, but H. joked "What's that, the neighbours? We haven't even started rehearsing!" I put down my bass and jogged to the windows – we could see the yellow-brick skyscraper on the other side of the narrow street, and I could almost spot the opposing sidewalk if I stood on my tiptoes, but we were on a floor too high to see all the way down to the pavement.

- This would make some badass concert hall, blabber-gabbled Sim, who had the easiest set up of all (and slowpoked about it), and had just finished when I got to the windows.

- It's just some riot in the street, I blurted, spotting the top of heads, what loomed as colons of angry demonstrators – a mob.

- Oh, articulated Ivan, whose tube amp had finished warming up, leading him to flip the distortion on.

- A mob? gulped Sim walking to my side.

- Yea, looks like it, shrugged I.

- That can't be good, he added.

The noise from the mob grew as loud as Ivan's guitar, so the good compadre that he is cranked the volume up. I went back to grab my bass when I heard some gunshot. I didn't turn around; I put the strap over my shoulder, and joined Ivan in a loose dive into *Requiem ad memoriam Albert Ayler*, from our first album. That song usually impressed people, because on that one H. revealed her third talent (after drumming, and owning a van): playing saxophone. On that song, she had figured out an easy drum part (kick and snare), so she could play saxophone simultaneously (multitasking to the max). Going into absolute free-form, it was also a tune where we sometimes switched instruments, ad lib, or where we other band mates would go back and bang on a few drums while H. was pulling that stunt. Ivan was pumping the groove, and I chromatically stretched my fingers over it, dropping in and out of the main hymn, until H. hollered to quit it, because she was still assembling her drum set. We put our amps on standby; Sim hailed us to the windows.

At that time, we noticed that without our jamming, the noise from the alleys had grown vicious. "This can't be good", Sim stated matter-of-factly.

-   Relax, they aren't rioting in The Rails, grunted Ivan.

-   They're shooting, Sim whimpered.

The cacophony of screams grew louder, we could just make out heads, hats, helmets, running...

Just then, K. arrived late-not-too-late, her thin blonde hair hanging off her shoulder in a mermaid-tail braid, a friend along her side to help her carry her gear. K. always brought more that the rest of us. One could say, she was the most professional amongst us (or that she just enjoyed gear too much). There were times, with Sim, where we wondered why she bothered sticking with our band, since she obviously was better, and could have toured with any actually famous musician if she so desired. We figured she stayed in the band because we were the only ones who didn't bore her (we did keep things interesting; that was the faith of our band: we did something interesting, new; we did something different, we weren't a banal band). Ivan greeted her with a "They didn't shove their arms too deep down your asses when they searched you?", and she grinned and panted "actually, they x-rayed us". She wiped the sweat off her brow as she set down her stuff.

She had her usual equipment. One pluggable archtop guitar she had modified herself with salvaged parts, for a really dark tone (or rather, no-tone). She had owned it for eons, and had favoured it among her collection for as long as I had known her. In the other case was her new pride and joy, though Ivan had deemed it "overkill", and that most of what she had put in was useless. She had responded by tagging him as a *brand snob*, who had no idea how to properly handle his Rickenbacker, and adding "next guitar I make, I'll make with a Valvebucker just to piss you off" (though the rest of us knew she'd do it, but not just to piss him off). This day when K. came in, Ivan kept quiet, to my relief (I despised petty quarrels); it came to mind I should thank him for not raising a fist at K..

"Brand snob" was the opposite of K.. She was a gearhead, and knew quality not by how it was called, but by how it was built. I had always seen her jamming on no-name, or lesser-known name instruments (in a general trend, modified). Originally trained as a woodworker, she had moved towards a luthier's craft: that was how she made a fine living, retaining a solid reputation despite the crash of every market around, each surprise-predicted recession.

In any case, this new pride she had revealed in our recording sessions, and she called "Vanilla sound" (she wanted the sound to be smooth, flavourful, and bright, like vanilla; K.'s weakness had always been picking out names and titles: the ones she thought up were pretty bad... just like this one, which I didn't care for). The guitar finish was *Cream Burst*, harmonizing into brown contours and back (vanilla/crême brûlée theme). A 7-string guitar, the body was oval shaped (lengthwise). Made from Tigerwood with a Purpleheart fretboard, the 27-fret u-profiled neck was a thick fatback (unusual for a lead guitarist's choice, but K. said she wouldn't trade in the extra deep *oomph* a thick neck gave, and that it didn't hinder her fast playing). The fretboard had a compound radius, starting at a soft 8, going down to an 11, small movable frets to play microtones (she praised sustain, and felt playing fretless had too little sustain, even if the neck was plated, like some vintage Vigiers were), and glow-in-the-dark side marker dots, and no inlays (they wouldn't have been compatible with the movable frets). The short and only slightly inclined headstock (the truss rod adjusted at the heel – though she claimed it would never have to be adjusted), was rounded like a half-moon, and the locking tuners spread all around the top, giving a crown-like appearance. It was heavily equipped – a lipstick pickup at the neck, followed by some strange three-rail pickup of her own design, one ultra-hot Lace sensor type pickup, a telephonic p-90, and a wide over-wrapped ceramic humbucker at the bridge (itself, a large cam operated vibrato system). On the lower side of the guitar were 5 stacked volume-in-tone knobs (one for each pickup), allegedly made from recycled sea-salvaged plastic. Behind the bridge were individual on-off slider switches for each pickup (which could slide in either direction to put pickups out-of-phase), and individual three-position tone switches also. The three position switches worked with the tone knobs in the following way – switched upwards was a bypass where a pickup's tone was at 100%, switched to the middle, the tone was whatever the tone knob was set to, and switched down, the tone was at 0% (a tone-kill). Thus, the possibility of toggling relatively rapidly between sounds, and presetting tones on specific pickups in advance. There were two other buttons, that you push-pulled to activate, that exposed the noise-rock destiny meant for *Vanilla sound*: one that un-cancelled the hum (as she had made the three single coils hum-cancelling on a normal basis, unless the button was pulled, if she wanted the 60-cycle grizzle – don't ask me how that worked); the other was a "feedback friend", as she called it (it boosted or reduced feedback, if she wanted to play with it). If that wasn't enough, the tremolo bridge had a built-in mute (she didn't care about palming if she didn't have to), and a trigger to putt the E into drop-D, and the 7th D into drop-B or back again. Though I wasn't a guitar player, I admired K. for this versatility-infinite instrument she had concocted to her taste, to make her job ever more intricate (she had a set list with tone controls for each song memorized, just to get the most out of her new brainchild), and I did think Ivan was just jealous. Great musician as he was, he never would have the patience, interest, or insanity to go as far as K. who, she, hurt herself to make her job harder and expansive (if her strives were even worth the toil). She always sounded brilliant, avidly hunting for ultra-specific tones which she heard in her head, and perhaps truly achieved only half the time. Sounds that no one else could recognize. She would be frustrated if she had a bit too much twang here, or if her pickups sounded "plunky". We agreed that with a mediocre sounding instrument you could still make amazing sounding music, but she wouldn't settle for that. The heart desires what the heart desires, I suppose. And when she'd wish to relax, ache for a simpler existence, she'd switch to her simple partscasted archtop.

Her friend – we all knew her, she played violin in another band, and occasionally jammed with us, though she obviously hadn't planned to at that time, as she didn't carry her fiddle – set down the amp and the archtop, and K. set the bag containing her pedal board, and took the gigantic case she had built for the very long *Vanilla sound* down from her back. Their cheeks were red and they were sweating from the weight carried up multiple flights of stairs (I had just stopped perspiring myself).

-     With that thing, why d'you need the archtop? Razzed Ivan snidely.

-     Wouldn't you like to know, K. remarked, insinuating he knew less than she.

Not wanting them to get into another "my guitars are better, and I play better than you" argument, I stepped in, demanding "One day, I have to get you to build me a bass, K.".

-     I'll put in a mudbucker, she stated; or that legendary monster from the Ovation Magnus, she laughed; I'll finally move you away from single coils, get you a truly *bassy* tone, but I'll have to make it vintage-ish for you: that's all you ever look at; I'll stay away from the millennial-turn sound.

-     That's almost all that's worth to look at! Won't be too hard for you, obviously. We swim in similar waters.

-     No offence though, I wouldn't mind giving you something a little more versatile than that old Bulgarian bat. We can't say it ever was high quality.

-     Offence taken! I declared half jokingly; when it works so well after all those years? And it has such a mellow low-output voice... and have you ever seen such a beautiful girl? Okay, the action on the high frets is a little high, and her neck is a little thin... I'm used to the thin neck, some like it, I like it, and I don't... maybe I wouldn't be against something wider. Or something with 5 strings?

-        I'll have to make it very good looking to be forgiven, won't I? Seriously, it could be fun. I can't believe we haven't talked about this before. And I have no projects after the launch. No one has projects these days... I'll surprise you!

-        Don't be mad if I still play my Hebros after, though.

Our banter was broken off by Sim, yelling for us to shut up. He had remained near the windows, sky reflecting on his bald knob, but was now crouching down close to the floor. I hadn't noticed the noise growing deafeningly loud from below. Isn't it fascinating how, at times when we are so focused on specific elements – for instance, K.'s ardency –, we acquire the ability to shut out the rest of the world? That swelling white noise, growing heat, degree upon degree, we don't notice until at last we suffocate bloodshot flushed-faced. Going from dark basement to bright sunlit outdoors hurts the eyes, but progressively absorbing light increased, we can forget the change, stare unblinking into the sun as to forget or confuse white light or pitch blackness, blinded by habit. Love is a much cited example of this effect, forgetting the world as we remain focused, that is (long googly-eyed staring into the beloved's soul, as the universe could come to an end, crashing down around and on those blissful consciousnesses, so entirely focused they became absent). Of course, I did not love K. – we had known each other for too long, in too many an image-shattering situation for that ever to happen, and I loved my partner – though we did have this intense fondness in our friendship, that, at times, can rival love in how much we feel and care for the other, I think.

It was too bad she and Ivan – who too was a dearest of friends – often fell at each others' throats. Once H. said to me that the most important thing we could do to keep the band going, was to ensure Ivan and K. kept on getting along; I told H. that I thought two things could be done to achieve this. The first: have them take more drugs together. The second: find ways to get them to rely on each others' strengths, rather than being jealous. "Is that possible thought, them being so prideful?" she asked. "If we get them drunk enough", I replied. Drugs, drunk, get them properly smashed to smash their jealous egos. I should have added a third thing: make sure they never succumb to attraction, or affection. Granted, they were both attractive (as far as I could tell, me being a bad judge, and not saying they were attractive for each other, but in general regards, they had pretty attributes). But if they were to fondle each other, fury lashing out sexually, as it feels (and can feel) good... *Love* and jealousy is a highly unstable and explosive combo.

So, at that moment, after K.'s arrival had abducted of our attention, and when talking with her had replaced the void-like immense room around me, and the murmurs of the cosmos, Sim shrilled for us to shut our pie-holes, and added "Large gatherings in the streets aren't possible now... only in crowd controlled events... what is?...".

— Can't be something too bad, gun shots and all, scoffed Ivan; now, we have to practice.

— They're shooting, man! cried Sim.

— We saw them on our way in, what d'you say it was, avouched K., addressing her friend.

— I didn't say for sure. Just, I heard about some people who wanted to show they weren't happy with most things being closed down, they want more freedom to move around, they doubt any conflict will actually erupt.

Sim pointed down at the street, I forget what he was mumbling and at the same time, Ivan had tossed a glance my way. He was raising his eyebrows up and down, had pinched his lips, his eyes darted from one end of the room to another. I came closer to him and sat on his amp. I whispered something along the lines of "You know, I think it's good that you don't care about K.'s new guitar. She changes her sound all the time, looks for so much versatility, it gets to be like quicksand. She's a virtuoso in her own right, but a lot of those virtuosos just go so all-out, that in the end, you're left with nothing. You can't enjoy it, because there's no ground. You may shred a panoply of mind-blowing solos, lengthy complex melodies, but maybe everyone'd like something to remember the tune by, you know? You and I, we give solidity to the band. I don't think I ever told you I think the rick-o-sound stereo slays on a rhythm guitar. I know we won't have it during practice, but at the gig tonight, it'll be huge. Just to bring back the idea of 12 string again, 12 string was Rickenbacker's flagship."

–　　I don't get why she brought that archtop, he grunted.

–　　Well... think of it this way, if you get that fretless Eastwood, you won't use it for every song? Our means have made us modest, but it used to be very common for musicians to have 3 or even 4 guitars they'd use on stage... For bigshots... Even more... I pondered with somewhat of a sour taste in my mouth – sour both in long-expired nostalgia from those days when an artist could make a decent living, play concerts often, when clubs were everywhere, when people would go out to concerts casually instead of surfing (as especially the older generation did) an infinite continuum of cheap and industrially produced *home entertainment* (an acquired taste that reflected on the individuals as one became what one "ate", or better said, "consumed"), and secondly because after those intended compliments, all that Ivan could think of was jealousy; come to think of it, maybe a primal motive was that K. earned a better living than the rest of us (though frankly, if the industries had been better regulated, Ivan and myself could have earned decently as session musicians...).

–　　Yea...

–　　Hey, I thought you liked where you lived, rambled I (my mind had taken a short cut from jealousy, to income, to Ivan's apartment)

    –   I like that I can live there, he said, not noticing anything strange with my question; I like how it lets me live.

He smiled at me, when H. had finished mounting her drum set, banging on the snare, trying out the harsh reverberations of the high ceiling. Ivan flicked his amp from *standby* to *on* and ripped out the riff from *icicle xylophone*. Coincidentally, the power went out, leaving only H.'s snare, mingled in with the mob ruckus, featuring the more and more frequent pang of gunshots.

    -    The fuck's wrong with you? Sim Bellowed harshly.

    -    What? I'm supposed to interfere? Queried Ivan, pointing at the windows.

15

Power had been cut, phone lines were out, signals were weak when not blurred. That's all we knew. We freaked out, until we got in touch with the people at The Rails who grudgingly admitted that they had no power either, and that they were forced to shut down. In other words, the show was cancelled, and we were literally in the dark. We hung out in the penumbra, flipping shit, with bursts of boom-boom death-stick and shattering resonating in the streets, on the opposing side of the glass. Our first idea was to dig into the food supplies we had with us – bread, smoked tofu, tomatoes, and the likes. Our second decision was to get high. I had enough for everyone in my bass case; we put small doses of Ecstasy into rolling paper and swallowed those parachutes, and then we lit up a couple of joints. Before we had swallowed the *chutes*, I stood up for a toast: "Friends, the good thing about impending catastrophe and major conflicts, regardless about how little we care for that BS, is that although everything *normal* becomes an enormous pain, no one gives a damn about the formerly taboo, and drugs are easier and easier to come by. To all our troubles, some appeasement."

K., her lean triangular thin-lipped and long-lashed visage staring at her vape, waiting for it to warm up, looked particularly glum about the show, bellyaching about "*Vanilla sound*'s" repealed grand stage debut, swallowing large gulps of the ginger soda we had cleverly packed (knowing we should keep a bottle handy for the eventually of our consuming psychedelics), in order to ease her parachute down, and feel less queasy when it would dissolve in her stomach. Ivan was puffing on a joint he had rolled while I had prepared the ecstasy; he'd rather inhale doobies over steam as, in his word, "some folks just need that smoke". He had always had a hard time getting high, and so, didn't do it often. His income and gusto for *fineries* were contributing factors, but usually, if he did seek to become entranced, he was more of an acid eater. He really needed strong hallucinations to take off. The theory I had developed when we were younger than we were at that point (since we weren't in our thirties yet, except for Sim who was a bit older and was sporting a sexy 32), was that Ivan was too intelligent to be really susceptible. Too intelligent might not be the right choice of words – he was differently intelligent than K. for example, or Sim who was the most business savvy of the band. Ivan was in touch with existence in another way, in a very personal way. He had no doubt about our connection to the material plane, he understood how things worked immediately. I think that's also why at some point, he stopped caring about a lot of it. Unlike me – I never really cared for other peoples' nonsense – he just gave up on watching the news, having political discussions, going to rallies... He still voted, but that was more or less it. He used to talk tons with people about what went down in the world – I remember zoning out of discussions he had with his sister, who I flirted with for a long time until I accepted that she just thought I was a freak. But eventually he declared "Am I the only one who understands anything?" He gave up. He was on another level of understanding how society worked, but witnessing said society spoiled rancid with absurdity (I recall him getting irritated at people who established non-correlations, linked topics that weren't related; I thought one name he had for it – *whataboutism* – was hilarious), he didn't want to understand anymore. I guess he started getting high more regularly at that point, but still a lot of drugs didn't have that strong of an effect on him.

We were seated on the ground, in a circle, with only the building's vague, dim, emergency lighting to set the sole mood available in our concert's stead. After the first joint had gone round, H. excused herself to the bathroom, though we wouldn't see her for the half hour to come (we made a lot of masturbation jokes at her expense). I didn't realize it when the ecstasy kicked in, I just know that at one point K.'s friend remarked "wow, look at your eyes!" The odd notion of attempting to stare into my own eyes made me laugh at first, but she had a small mirror which she pulled out of her bag; hilarity amplified by my misunderstanding, I had trouble holding the looking-glass straight, such intense giggles persisted. I could see, myself, in the murk, two black holes substitute my sockets; sufficient information to know my pupils were ridiculously dilated. I considered how I was feeling, and concluded I had no anxiety, I had no dark thoughts, no anger. I felt completely happy, even though all we had prepared for, all our hype, was for nothing. We had no album launch, we had no way of knowing if we could play in other cities, other locations, if we could step out of this tower, to sum up, we had nothing, but I was happy. What was this earthquake which marooned us in this standing pile of rubble, this building left to decay? Nothing worse than what we had had to deal with in the past. Nothing worse than the time Sim got hit by a car at a two day's drive beyond our borders where we didn't have any insurance... We'd find another date for our album launch, I felt happy. Seeing myself made me realize how I felt. I saw a physical representation of my emotions. To better know myself, I had to see myself. I was like those people who had to dress very snazzy, with bright colours, soft fabrics, in order to know, themselves, how they were. Unlike zealots tend to believe, it wasn't vanity – I was happy about myself, but I reminded myself I was happy. I thought about how girls who "make themselves pretty" don't always do it out of vanity, narcissism or fashion (though many do), but to try to add beauty to their vicinity, or remind themselves, through their own selves, of the beauty in the world. I set the mirror down. K's friend was very pretty, and I felt like dancing with her. She reminded me of what was pretty in the world. I said to K., "your archtop still plays without juice, why don't you give us some entertainment?", taking K.'s friend by the hand, bringing her to her feet.

Sim was morose, he vocalized they were still shooting out there. "They want to kill each other, let them do it. They can leave us alone to dance", I hailed, putting my arm around K.'s friend's waist. K. strummed a few chords, and went into the jazz standard *Alone together*. And that was a perfect choice. It was, for we were alone together away from all that was going wrong, that I didn't care for, that I never cared for, I didn't even know why tensions were escalating – at the borders, elsewhere, on Mars for all I spat upon –, and I was proud not to know, because it was a load of bullcrap, and a waste of time, and not knowing was the best weapon. Not knowing what racism is, not knowing what sexism is, are the best tools against those, as you have no way to imagine such stupid concepts. I didn't know what their conflict was, I think Ivan didn't either, I think K. had the *jist* of it. What did we care? We played music, we danced. Music was more important to the world. We were in a whispered world, our own theatre. I recalled seeing a play, *Someone came to come* where they repeated in a dreamy way, over and over, "We are alone. Together alone. Alone together.", a rather old play by a foreign author. I was happy, I was dancing. I don't know what I was seeing, my eyes were enchanted by the glimmers of lights reflected here and there in the room, reflected here and there were flashes, and, and blaring roars. Sim said they were still shooting at each other. "Use it as a beat", I told K..

Sim's *medication* wasn't taking effect. He was sad, wouldn't stop ranting about how we shouldn't have released the album, how in this time period, we shouldn't have released anything, we shouldn't have done anything, we should have waited, that this album was going to fall way under the radar, be forgotten, maybe all the master tapes would be destroyed, the physical copies, non-physical copies, the fully undivided shebang was going to be destroyed. Ivan looked him straight in the face, and said "You think you should grow a moustache?" I remember this, I wanted Sim to have a good time, as much of a good time as I was having close to K.'s friend, who smelled marvelously sweet (I had never realized this, in all the times we had jammed together, because we had never been this close, except for once maybe, when the whole band plus her, we all had decided to crash on a single couch, after drinking a bottle of rum, so we all smelled to an equal degree of sweat and alcohol), and whose body was very warm. Our faces were at equal height, which made it difficult to be drawn away from her soft cheeks and her lips; we were swaying, and moving in a manner which conferred we both felt weightless, and each touch made our organs expel their crippling tension in a feverishly delectable breath (or so, it appeared for her just as for me); I thought of how pleasant it was to have the attention of a woman, even if it should go nowhere, if it meant nothing, how great it was to have this connection, this validation. I knew I had issues, that I needed exterior validation from girls who in all my *apprenticeship years* as some call *youth*, treated me as a plague-ridden *freak* (though I was a kind of freak, except for me that was a good thing). I thought about the changes I had undergone in my life – trying to work out, dress better, speak better, make fewer crude jokes – which hadn't worked at all (therefore, in turn, I returned to making crude jokes, and cursing, which I learned was only the way most adults spoke; those adults tell young people not to talk that way, and some young people listen, view said behaviour as *improper*, only to start speaking that way when they would turn 20, 25, getting *worse* with age). And I wished I didn't crave this attention from the opposite sex, nonetheless, I did, and it was very satisfying to get it, as I thought of my partner all this while, who so lovingly supported my music career.

Ivan's question only in part distracted Sim; he subsequently had the noids even more so: "What the hell are you asking about a moustache when the world is turning to shit and we might all die tonight for all it's worth and everything we've ever done is worthless and...", Ivan cut him off by grabbing him by the collar and kissing him straight on the mouth. Both were heterosexual, but Ivan had a habit of kissing people to get them to shut up – it wasn't the first time he had smooched Sim. I remember the first time he kissed Sim, was when Sim was losing his shit because a cheap rental car's engine had burst, and we were going to be late for a gig; Ivan *pucked him up*, and shouted "We'll be late man. We're gonna figure it out. We're a rock band, we'll be *fashionably late*". Sim perplexed had surveyed "Hmm, do all guys kiss so differently from women?" (Sim had seen Ivan pull the move before, accounting for the mild surprise). (And yes, Sim had real bad luck when it came to cars; maybe on account of him over stressing so much). This time, referring to his own whiskers, Ivan asked "D'you like how it feels on your lip?" Sim finally relaxed, admitting "eh... yea!"

How time elapsed is unknown to me. This was to be foreseen, with what had been ingested. Eventually H., K. and Ivan cooked up tunes together, H. using empty containers and the likes to avoid making too much noise, and Ivan jamming on my Hebros, which we couldn't hear so well, but which still sounded, given it was a hollow-body. Sim was laying on his back – I recall seeing him palping his face, and mostly his lips, for a long while. Myself and K.'s friend, were leaning against the biggest window, peering into the street at times (it had mostly quieted down), and holding each other. She was leaning onto me, I was holding her, she was holding me. Ecstasy fascinated me in its capacity to emphasize, or articulate, every positive feeling, everything that's good, and nice, in astounding simplicity. Resounded in my head, this notion that it might as well be over, that trains won't run, that roads will be blocked, that buildings will be bombed. That every day would serve the purpose of waiting a return to minimal sanity.

In front of my eyes, the room shimmered in geometric patterns anew renewed. I saw the city's profile, envisioned it on walls and ceilings. Many criticized (or blandly repeat the criticism they'd heard floating about) the rust-brown coloured high-rises – mostly the ones that emerge in the bullseye of our metropolis, and stretch out highest over our panorama. Would they really have preferred the ordinary grey-and-glass of most millennial-turn structures? Or the concrete of old? To me, there was beauty in each of these – could be, at least – and I liked the rust-brown coloration of this capital. It looked like some aged machine, fallen into disuse (that which it almost was). All those people who bashed this old wreck, they didn't actually look at the city as a place where people lived. They looked at it as a place of business, a place where you would tear down what was built last week. Because aimless destruction and reconstruction was good for business, somehow. The burning of wealth, in some deranged equation, corresponded to the creation of wealth. They looked at the city as an automaton, where robots performed undying nonsensical labour before returning to their ready-assembled ikea suburbs. No, they didn't see a city as a place where people lived. Who lives? Who cares? None of them walked the streets. Who were they? Did we really know? Did they know? Or no one knew, like none of them knew what a city looked like. Perhaps those who do live in it, and walk the streets, and go to concerts, and exhibitions, and bars where people talk with each other in between drinking alone, and discuss the movies they just saw after walking out of movie theatres, or the plays they just saw after walking out of regular theatres, instead of brushing off their impressions like they don't matter, or flirt, or dance, or get randy in the bathroom, or wait for dates that stand them up, or get drunk for the hell of it. Then again, I did that, and I didn't know what a city looked like either – I thought it looked like a heap of rusting metal. I knew a city only by its sounds, which was maybe more than what most people knew it by. Or by the way it thrives...

Sounds... sounds... the glimmering I saw about the room expanded in those occasional flashes accompanied by sudden blasts, and those blaring echos, they weren't the sounds of a city. Repeated gunshots have no place in the soundscape of a city – they are what turn a city into a battleground. A battleground can't be a living city, because no one can live there without first thinking of it as a battleground. At this boundary, chasm, conception of our surroundings, were we stuck in this building – we started talking about it "we'll be here overnight, won't we?" Was going out possible? It would have meant getting stuck in some bullshit conflict. Conflicts have this way of not taking in anyone's opinion. You can't walk through it saying "Nope, I'm not in this, this doesn't have anything to do with me". The conflict comes to you. Else people could have come to our concert – we didn't want conflict, most people certainly didn't either. Yet, our concert was cancelled, and we were locked in this place in order not to get senselessly shot. In the daylight, we guessed we would perhaps be able to leave, to go... somewhere? We had no idea, no idea of anything anymore. I was happy though, I felt so happy, so well – holding K.'s friend, this evening. It was nice, we were in another world. I availed in not dwelling on what could have been – unlike Sim, who still wasn't able to let go – and to enjoy what *was*. And cities, living or dead, past, never to be seen standing the same again, reduced to ruins, or shimmering in only a single beholder's eyes – rejoicing through the uncertainty about which I would succeed in not giving a damn – I reached my right hand up to gently brush K.'s friend's cheek, her chin, to turn her head to the left, towards me, so that I could kiss her.

I thought of my partner who I would maybe not see again, and that I would never stop loving her, and I thought of the gunshots that detonated behind my back, right beneath us, K.'s friend and I, (and that could even break through the glass and kill me on the spot), and we kissed, and I felt happy. She pinched her lips, and confessed "You know, it always bothers me a little that you only call me *you*. I don't think I ever heard you call me by my name." So I responded "It's better if we don't get too personal. Maybe I can call you by part of your name?" "Part of my name?" "Yes. *El.*, I could call you *El*." "Wouldn't having a nickname for me that only you in the entire world call me by, make it even more personal than if you called me by my first name?... It's a very common name". "No... It's part of your name... it's only part as intimate." I clowned, before pulling her elongated body, and her triangular visage crowned by bangs of her fragrant brown hair; we started kissing again.

I heard snickering in the background, and Ivan divulged "who did I bet with, that *that* was bound to happen?" H.'s voice quipped "I think it was with his girlfriend." K's voice muttered "I don't know, but I owe you dinner."

16

We had no conception of what was happening as noises more deafening arose all around. The only obvious one was that of a helicopter. Sim had passed out gently, on his back, from stress and exhaustion. None of us, beside him, were going to sleep that night. We weren't going to sleep; it was a magical night.

Our lips grew numb, K's... *El.* and I. Her body was so light, like that of a bird. Her eyes also were large dark unbarred escapes, wormholes of our imagined cosmos, black holes into other dimensions, a dimension where we were. I forget about what we talked. K., H. and Ivan left to look at the rest of the building. El. and I stayed, leaning against one of the ceiling-high windows. Bliss flooded away the hours, as an overflowing river rips villages from their foundations, devastates harvests, inundates or irrigates farther into fields and forests, feeds the creatures that thrive in its delta.

At one point, the room seemed purple. I had been told purple (or violet, or mauve, or whichever shade derived from night) was the colour of dreams, and the unconscious. Sim told me that people who never remember their dreams, as they reject their unconsciousness, cannot tolerate the colour purple. My eyes went up and down the serpentine mouldings surrounding the base of the chandeliers hanging overhead. Eventually, I believed that dawn had come, because of a rising manifest brightness. As it appeared, it was due to the headlights of a couple of vehicles going down the street beneath us. So accustomed to the dark, and so sensitive were our eyes, that it had blinded us like the coming day for which there had been no preparing, for which it would have been impossible to prepare. And we laughed at our perception of time, irrelevant and distorted as it was, after we had mistaken a prolonged sunrise to be the minute-momentary rushing of machinery.

17

The others returned; Sim awoke. Ivan was perfectly lucid – the effects of the previous drugs had worn out, and he was bored. "When are we gonna eat shrooms?" he pleaded. El. and I arose, our legs stiff, as from the grave (interestingly enough, we used the same word for *there-from-which-there-is-no-return*, where some dead are left to decompose, and for that which is overly serious, saddening, distressing, and from where we would not return, souls unmutated, unchanged, yet in our case, resurrected by the divine; hadn't we kissed, would we have been left to putrefy?); we walked to them, they who had paced their temporary cage, we who had sunken into the comfort of each other, buried our spectres – our real form belonging to another realm, where they would have been welcome in their likes. K. was the one who had shrooms (she knew how to grow them, or rather, had spores), highly potent golden capped shrivelled fungi, of which she had brought a whole paper bag. I had no idea why she was packing, but she sure was. I looked at the bottle of ginger soda, and mentioned there wasn't much left; our stomachs would get woozy before we took off. We were on pretty empty stomachs too (our provisions had been minimal – not planned for an entire wake).

The fungi were stale, hard to chew, hard to swallow. I never minded the taste, though most people do. I loved mushrooms in general, and admitting these had a hash, bitter taste, they weren't too bad. The while we each ate, perhaps a bit more than the dose we normally would have, and looked forward to a fun few hours to come. That's when it came to me: "What about your van?" I tackled H. She replied "It's in the garage below ground. Waiting for a time when we can drive it out." "Shouldn't we put the instruments in the van before we begin seeing great things?" I inquired. "We still have long to bide by before sunrise; we'll be out of it before noon" K. assured us, "this batch didn't wax as potent." Sim was on the ground again, and was humming *High powered trance*, from our second album. I grabbed my bass, and plucked along with him.

I started feeling like such wimp; I was so hungry, yet I hadn't even fasted through the night. I did recall, from days on the road where at times, we didn't have a minute to get food between travel, gigs, arrangements, et cetera, that it was the first few hours of hunger that felt the most difficult. After a little while, hunger became not only tolerable, but at times, pleasant, refreshing (that was, before it came back even fiercer – and this, without ever seriously starving, though I had vaguely overheard that this conflict-thing some feared, meant potential mass starvation. But to hell with that). And I abhorred feeling wimpish, since life was something to be celebrated, and both my art and my purpose had a drive to celebrate life, that is also to push my individual character past barriers, defeat, lament and woe, and ridicule those around me who would rather bow in religious pretense, to priests exalting grim human sacrifice instead of song and dance. Pushing forward, not in harsh detriment of one's person, but pushing forward sensing one's muscles, one's spirit at work; overcoming difficulties as proof that one is alive and well – that is, song and dance over human sacrifice. Sacrifice is a finality – a head chopped off, a heart cut out, and death follows – song and dance are continuous rituals perpetrated when no rest or work are needed. When creation is at its pinnacle: liberated from burdens, able to enjoy itself, to cut loose.

To hell with the lot of 'em! Mass starvation! Mass starvation as a result of their "work"! To say, we once worked to have food, and now some fanatics are working to burn crops! To hell with the lot of 'em; I will not abase myself to their crud-level.

18

The trip which was to occur had absolutely nothing to do with the events of the day. Granted, obviously large parts I couldn't later recall, not for lack of memory, or out of sheer haziness, but because there was too much to recall, and contrarily to the effect of the ecstasy, most of it wasn't purely emotional; it was a larger, sensorial experience. All who've tried these substances know what I mean.

At first, just like with the fast-fading remnants of the previous trip, the world was shiny, splendid, and surfaces were divided into small triangular geometric patterns – gleaming spiderwebs. I was starting to believe that I was in a spiderweb – how *vampirical*, El. had been sucking my blood and soul, while I loved a woman, somewhere, in a part of the firmament cut-off from myself! I saw how the world was unnaturally cut up – a map at my feet to tread upon.

Tall, enormous, titan-like storm troopers, with blank faces, dressed in patchwork uniforms, made of bits of flags, bits of many coloured fabrics, insignia from what I guessed were battalions of many armies. Those Storm troopers were brandishing bayoneted riffles, and shooting, hitting, a mirror, which stood on the other side of a chalk line. Storm troopers on both sides of the mirror, of the chalk line, had finished building a brick wall, in the wall, had installed a huge vault, made of dark carbon steel, with a circular door – a vault the likes of which I had seen in caricatures, in cartoon banks. Looking away, there were more vaults along the wall, more groups of colossus legionnaires. They locked the circular vault doors, spun the wheel-locks round and round, and laughed while aiming gigantic cannons at opposite vault door. But then they stopped laughing, they scratched their chins. They couldn't talk – they had no language to themselves, but through their gestures I understood they were arguing on whether they should blow the vault before the ones in the mirror should. Near me, the one who had done the most shooting showed himself to be the leader, holding his bayoneted rifle, scratched his forehead, lifted up his officer's cap. From under his cap fell his hair – it was made of strands of newspaper clippings. I was running somewhere along the wall, and wanted to cross, pass through the door, to the inner-vault, or the other side of the wall, and the mirror-wall, but they closed the steel doors right in my face. I just wanted to walk. I wanted to walk to the city where I lived, with the girl I loved, but I couldn't, the road was closed. I said I wanted to walk, that I just wanted to walk through fields and forests, but they laughed. I understood they were saying no one could. They had decreed – NO WALKING! No walking was permitted, in fields, in forests... They were going to shoot me. They wanted to shoot me for walking where they had decided one wouldn't walk. I raised my arms to protect my face, but I heard laughing.

I snapped back to myself – of course I wasn't seeing any of that; I had had my eyes closed, it was a dream (perhaps I had been sleeping? Asleep through the trip?) – I wasn't standing on a map of the world, so small next to huge soldiers. But I did hear laughing – I looked about the penumbra; it was Sim. Sim was on his back, laughing his brains out, curling over, holding his guts, crying from laughter. But the laugh wasn't his: he was out of his mind, the laugh was a carnivorous beast that had pounced on him. It was a hyena, buff, of protruding muscles, with dark yellow fur, and mad eyes. One such varmint wanted me – it was a leopard-furred hyena, coming from a corner. Its fangs bared, mouth agape, drooling, cackling wack-delightfully. I was funny to it, stuck, famished, in this place. It had hunted me into this cavern. We would be hunted – I knew this. Even if we didn't go out into the war-torn, civil-distressed streets now, only to get shot by both parties, or caught by stray bullets (words yelled out in anger, violence left hanging by violence), all and the same it would catch us up, it would never leave us alone. I had ignored it, but I was being hunted, we were all hunted. I just wanted to play music, and be with people I enjoyed, but I was being pursued.

The beast stood on its hind legs, like a man, before returning to its rounded-back, sprinting position, and it pounced on me.

I raised my arms, and fell backwards. Surprisingly enough, I didn't hit my head; my head landed on K.'s lap. She was sitting, looking at the ceiling, and conferring with El. and Ivan. I hadn't noticed they were trialoguing. A loose bit of phrase springs to recollection, Ivan, in his lucid, conscious-minded episode (he never lost grasp of what was veracious or counterfeit in what he was experiencing) avowed "It's amazing how well the rabbits I imagine, are painting the walls in pink." K. had her noggin tilted back (I knew this, by the way I glimpsed her throat and chin), and countered "I hear rain, it's so refreshing." El. was sitting with them – she leaned over and started kissing me.

Warmth flooded my face, blood rushed in all of my extremities, my body would have vibrated, resonated with the universe (maybe it was resonating; my legs flailed around, that I'm sure of – they were kicking, and slipping about). The tingling was too intense. She was no vampire, she was the nurse, who had collected my beaten remnants. She was bringing me back to health. Old friendship, old tensions. Yes, she had always been breathtaking. I had never dared speak her full name – I wasn't comfortable doing so. She had always been there to make me feel good, valued, to embellish the heavens I inhabited, my surroundings. Thanks to her attractiveness, I knew what love was, for only in contrast to the feelings she evoked, did I know the height of the feelings I had for my partner. Yet, from my partner, my lifeline had been severed. I was a bastard, a nothing, who, by fear of falling from too high, had landed on El.'s storey; in our story, circumstance meant everything.

Rain... yes, I could hear K.'s rain, washing away the dust that had arisen; I felt it dripping on me, rushing over my skin, making my clothes heavier. I felt wet, I felt large-dropped lukewarm summer rain, brushing through my hair (or it might have been her soft fingers), and the hairs on my arms, and my chest. She emitted small animal noises, small, cute moaning sounds, while we kissed, while we looked at each other. K.

giggled to Ivan "What do I do? They're making out on my lap." Ivan mused "Make out with them", K. suggested "You'd make out with anyone", Ivan assailed "I never made out with you", and K. retaliated "that's because you never had to make me shut up." Ivan challenged her "There are times when I wanted to." K. changed the topic "It's nice, the rain." Ivan said "It's not raining", but K. ignored him.

These quips, enshrined in my psyche, since they hatched two compulsive thoughts, hurtling towards each other, like trains bound to crash and be annihilated by one another. The first was that I would have liked K. and Ivan being a couple, though it would have ruined the band probably, and I wasn't ready for it to be over; they were both two of my oldest and dearest friends, who I admired, and who had more in common than their bickering would allow them to comprehend, if it shouldn't devastate them, if I shouldn't in total frankness hope so. A love affair could turn their rivalry into a passionate game, where at the end of the day, only their partner's presence counts. The other thought was that it wasn't, in fact, raining. It wasn't. What was my feeling of wetness? I thought of my skin peeling off, my body becoming liquid. No, that couldn't be – even though that's how I saw myself, in the dark, staring El. in the eyes, feeling her warm breath – I thought "it must be my sweat then. I'm shivering from the tenderness of her kisses like some weird schmuck, and I'm sweating like a pig, like nothing more than a miserable fat tub of lard. I'm disgusting, and I must stink. I always smell. After gigs, I feel terrible. I bring baby wipes, rubbing alcohol, and cologne with me, just to rid myself of my acrid musky stench." She was kissing me, drinking my melting corpse, savouring it, and I was evaporating, becoming vapour, becoming vaporized, into a cloud of reek. (No, I couldn't stink so horribly if she remained, bestowing upon me her kisses; I must have been better than I believed.) My skin crawled. It wasn't raining – we were inside. Something else was falling from the ceiling, something ripping my flesh, to let out my pulsating bloodstream (and how pulsating – I felt it in my neck, temples, lips, and stomach, an oceanic tide, tugging back and forth). I looked to the sides when I had opened my eyes. Darkness, only darkness, dots, black dots, an infinity of black dots. They were fleas. Fleas were raining down. The pleasureful tingling in my limbs had become painful. I rose at once, startling my friends to an audible gasp.

The two thoughts had collided – two trains were lying in the wreckage, derailed. I was lying in wreckage (this building!). I had no choice but to explore the only real wreckage (the building, or me? Of course, the building). I held out my hand to invite El. to stand with me (when she stood, I saw the expression on her face, that of joy recently emerged from sorrow; I knew my rising had panicked her, had made her sad). I quizzled what there was to see in the rest of the tower. H. answered from afar that there was nothing. A few vacant rooms, bathrooms, staircases, and a lot of locked doors. "Can we go all the way to the top floor?" - yes, she said yes - "is there a view?".

I didn't wait for a reply. Pulling El. by the hand, we strode for the exit. She was against the idea, hypothesized we'd get lost. "Aren't we lost already?" I knew we were lost. Flees were gnawing away at my bones. I was gone, she was gone, we were never going to leave this place. The staircase had more lighting than the room in which we had been – emergency lamps hung at every flight. Bars of light burst from between the disjointed steps. Leaping over two, three at a time, it was clear they were prison bars. We were in a prison, we had always been in a prison. A vault, a wall, bars, customs, it was all the same. These bars though, we could leap over. I wanted to hop out of prison, fly over borders, walk to where I willed, holding the hand of who I fucking wanted to. I wanted to hold El.'s hand, I wanted to run over prison cells with her, and rise as high as we could to see the view of the burning city.

I knew it would be burning. To cinders, to ashes. I knew they would have destroyed it, those bastards. Who were the bastards? Anyone who joined up with destruction, anyone who supported the idea of destruction, anyone who listened to the news and shit their pants, crossing their fingers for the annihilation of their newly conceived nightmares (the news, raping innocent peoples' imaginations, repeating horror tales, spreading rumours like immature high schoolers – news of all sources, and of the lowest sources the worst; "citizen-reporters", "single-truth seekers", or "all-blamers", AKA "no-truth preachers", *conspirationists*, taking their time to broadcast their personal vision of the day's issues; who the fuck asked them?). Those bastards who didn't live in the city, who didn't see it as a living place – they saw a battleground, a place of business, buildings you could construct today and tear down tomorrow, for the highest bidder. I knew they were taring it down with cannons and bombs, and with *voluntary* conscripts, as voluntary as a servant can be, brainwashed, fed with propaganda. I followed no news, ate no propaganda. I was (and still am) a bassist, and a damned excellent one. I would challenge anyone who would say I wasn't one of the best in the country, whatever that meant. I'm not usually a braggart, but to hell with mandatory modesty, I get tired of not admitting pride in what I am. Even though the pay was shit – however arts sold, with the ease we had to produce recordings, duplicate them, as true fame was black market fame, and as shows meant variable income when one got shows – playing music was what I cared about, and no hearsay about possible *rebellions* or *invasions*, or *war*, or *doom*, or *secret police*, or *spyware*, or *unexplained detentions*, or wispish pishposh, and what our rights should be, or not be, or become, was going to distract me from what was really important, god dammit: living, and having passion. I held El., I told her we would see the explosions that were turning streets into scars. She shook her head. She said we were above all that. That we weren't going to participate in any of it. That we were going to play music, that she wanted to play with our band. She said we were above it, not in this tower, but from the start, we were above it, and even though the album release failed, the fact that it had been planned, that *life* should have happened, that nothing stopped the living city, the living country, that nothing scared us into sewer tunnels, cowering away from ardour, was a victory (the only victory that would matter). We had won, she told me. Her eyes were wide open, we had won! We celebrated: we had won!

While we held each other, I had my eyes closed. I saw more colours than when they had open been. Her breathing was heavy. Since she was smiling, it sounded almost like hissing. Almost like she was crying. Was she crying out of joy? I opened my eyes, the whole staircase was lined black and yellow, and her face was crinkled, tearing, painful. She wasn't humming out of joy anymore. I kissed her cheeks, I kissed the tip of her nose, and her lips. Her face was salty with teardrops and the down-streaming rivers they sourced, before they should drip into her lap. I held her close and hummed a song, I hummed *Mannequins waltz stilly*, the romantic, soft-rock slow off our first album, which I had co-written, and still liked a lot. I held her firmer against my bony chest, and harder. I knew why she was crying – if we had won, why were we locked up, locked away, fearing the now forbidden outdoors?

Under my eyelids I marvelled at a faded reel of the first show I had ever played in. Back then, I played in a heavy metal band. It was in that weird lapse of time where renaissance outfits had become fashionable, though not everybody wore them. I had my first bass – I didn't know in those days, that what I really loved were vintage warm tones – a basic Yamaha bass, the model I can never remember (one of those with a serial number for a name – good basic instruments). The show was in a bar, at night. I was the youngest one in the band, "Disciples of chaos". the guitar player and drummer had put the band together as a fun, yet nothing-serious pastime. They were the old metalhead types, who liked to drink too much beer to build up their *Molson Muscles*, keep their long hair greasy, and tell each other fart jokes. The drummer had worked as a roadie for a few years, and taught me tons about gear, and the guitarist worked as an AV tech at a local college. Their lack of any type of pretense came from knowing they were passably mediocre musicians who could never have cut it professionally, and from being content with their routine fate. They had recruited these two nice girls to sing and play keyboards, but after a little under half a year of playing both girls quit the band, because they felt the older guys had only invited them to join so that they could ogle their keisters and budding boobies (and in fact, they were right about the middle-aged pervs). Both girls and myself, we made up another garage band – I played with both groups for that remaining year of high school, investing in them the entirety of my time, and L., one of those singers, became my first girlfriend. It was in that second band that the guitar player loaned me her Fender Mustang bass, and I found what kind of sound I was drawn to. That was another season of living...

But during that first concert those girls were still playing with the Disciples of chaos. L., combining Neo-renaissance trends and a throwback rocker chick look wore skinny, fake leather pants, some sort of embroidered shirt, topped with loose chainmail. I was dressed in black, with a new Gambeson (to my regret by how hot and weighty it was), and pushed heavy fuzz through my amp. I think that for the whole show, I didn't even go close to the front of the stage. The guitar player shredded best he could on a Gold Top Les Paul, the keyboard was grooving slow and ambient. Staying in the back, I never had projectors in my eyes, and could see the room well. I remember spotting a group of guys going through the front door, to the bar, and instead of ordering, leaning on the counter, looking at us, actively listening. We only played covers, not so well at that, yet that group of strangers, who leaned in, out to party, have a good time, had been cut in their tracks by our performing. That was perhaps the moment when I first felt a life purpose to play music, until my body should be animated no more. It would be my way to make society better, to be useful. On a daily basis, what makes peoples' lives better, in our day and age? Very few things, if you ask me. Music is certainly one of those reaching out to people, and stirring their feelings, and giving a reason to keep going. That concert lasted a cool hour, bathed in monotone yellow light, and by the end, I had grown more as a person than during the few years of schooling and routine that had preceded.

Playing heavy metal had been an immensely positive experience in my life, though I hadn't gone back to the genre in eons, nor had I acquired a bass predestined for the genre (not that aggressive pickups and such were *necessary* to play metal, a player was inclined towards it); the closest was my old Yamaha. Metal is a broad genre – should we compare speed, or thrash, to doom metal, or folk metal to Nu metal – yet in each of these sub-genres, one is required to learn precision in order to play melodic lines powerfully articulated (okay – not in Black Metal). Metal came forward with the perfection of high output, very sensitive pickups, which would retain a clear sound, with little to no feedback, at ear-bleeding volume, stacked with gain and effects. In such, though I barely listened to metal anymore (we ventured into hard stuff, but nothing which would have qualified as metal), it had done me good to delve into a genre that wasn't *mine*.

That concert came back to mind – I saw it, under my eyelids –, how there was no tech (only our amps, miked into a crummy soundboard connected to some old speakers the bar owned), no lighting variations, bad acoustics, and how overall we weren't great (our drummer was the only *seasoned* – or passable – player among us), yet how it affected me marvellously, this contact with another *self*, or an expansion of myself, or modified self, however it was. The salty taste on my mouth for the first time, my moist skin overflowing from my upper lip, the focused haze...

I was begging El. to stop crying in this murk of ideas, souvenirs, visions, strange lighting, and strange situations. I had to console her, and I felt again, myself doing something which wasn't me. What was I consoling her for? Everything was stupid. Everything was useless. I told her, the only thing that was real was where we were, and who we were, and what we did or wanted to do. Who we are is what matters. The idea of her crying, when we were going to play more music, was preposterous. We would be able to play again, to hear music being played. In our large hall, a few storeys lower, we could play as we had played, on unplugged instruments. What were we cowering for?

I took her by the hand, recalled we hadn't been to the top. But we didn't need to go to the top. What for would we want a long distance, unrealistic vision from high up? It wasn't from up there that the city pulsated, stirred, and that we chose our destinies. It was from down below, where we came from, where we went about our day-to-day realities. Had other peoples' conflicts kept us from "there over", that plain where action was manifest? Had it really been so, that we were locked up, because others had decided to fight, kill, obliterate? We had no reason to cower, when they were the ones who should be ashamed. We had a right to roam freely, stand proud, when we were at peace with people, and had more purpose than that of large-scale first-degree murder, if it should even happen. Was it happening? Probably. It happened everywhere. Folks everywhere were perpetually killing each other. Was that a reason for stopping ourselves from being happy? What if it should happen on a large scale? We had no reason to respect, obey, or glorify, any militaristic authority. El. was staring into my pupils – that watery, red-eyed, courageously terrified gaze of hers (for she had the bravery to envision the worst, even as we should have shut it out, she had the bravery to cry about it, and the courage to care) – and after clearing her throat, and wiping her face with her other hand, she quoted "*As my candle let itself be consumed into extinction, in the liquefied pool of its fragrant sanguine wax, I breathed, sleepless, into a dawn in which I would let myself become extinguished, if only in my own self and nature, rather than to betray the flame lighting the wick at my core in a pursuit for more darkness to light*: O. Kirjanen, in *A purpose at dawn*".

I told her "I recognize it... I read it, most have... it's a wonderful book... I was never really able to make out its meaning." She squinted and reckoned "It's very mixed... it can be... one or the other, if the character is right or... in the end, I think... you have to know what is his purpose at dawn...". "And what do you think? Us? Are we here only to light the evening, the night, or..? We will breathe, sleepless, into a dawn...". She leaned in "Ask me tomorrow evening", and commanded a long pause, gazing away, before tallying "I'm sorry. I didn't mean to cry. My high dropped a little. I'm no longer elsewhere. My emotions are bared. Bared wires. I have a crushing sense of reality... just a little."

We hadn't been to the top, and the idea that we needed to go down-below, where *living* took place, obsessed me. I got her to her feet and grabbed her hand to drag or lead her the whole way nether the staircase, to the outer egress. There, the fear of being locked out prompted me to find a trashcan, to prompt the door ajar, while we tiptoed out into the night air.

19

Strangely enough, the night was warmer than the day had been. As my skin had erupted into goosebumps during the chilly afternoon (waiting, in the powerless, unheated, large hall), my senses were now profuse, luxuriant as vegetation in the right climate burgeons into thick jungles. I beheld (my vision half blurred by fatigue, and distorted by substances – at the pallid moon fore which clouds fluttered) their silver moth wings lively with shades of dark. Somewhere in the distance, detonations resounded, rumbling in the ground, a rhythmic thump, Morse messages sent to remind us about potential or probable forthcoming... fuck it.

The ground glistened. Had it rained? El. told me that of course it had, hadn't I heard, or noticed? I wasn't sure.

Like the previous day, the rain had roused nature's aromas – a wonderful autumnal shift from the dry air we had huffed in the previous months of summer. A summer of heated stagnant air, devoid of moisture, that had suppressed scents, and had seared the sensation of every jaunt to the same singed bister tint the grass had assumed – before these recent showers, it had been as if no pleasant fragrance had ridden the winds since the linden trees had been in bloom. Large inhalations and exhalations restored a feeling of peace to my tingling guts. El. had quick, nervous breaths.

The avenue we waltzed into was empty. It was the one on the opposite side of our main quarters, or feasting hall (however one wishes to look at it), in the sky-scrapper that had serve as our refuge, in regards to the window we had leered out of; the avenue was wider on this side. Empty. The avenue was empty. Only here and there, remained laying on the asphalt a piece of cloth, a fragment of metal (a rod? A screw? A nut?), a shard of wood... There were no gunmen, no tanks, no villains, no big bad wolf. I wondered how far we could have gone like this, and started down the street. El. called my name, called it again. She ran to catch my arm, and tugged. There was rumbling in the ground, yet, around us, it was still.

20

Similarities with evenings at home; the muffled buzzing of far-off engines, urban glow, the breeze. City silence, the disconcerting beauty of metropolitan restlessness, nature disfigured into our stone tunnel cave-like homes of old – we Cro-Magnons –, laid out under an open sky. And at home, my girlfriend and I would gaze from our windows into the curfew flushed streets, civic hush harshly enjoyable – there was a curfew in my city, each city did, only the larger metropoles of our border-corral went to bed later (some assholes had calculated it was safer this way). Another similarity: the "sleep-over parties" that had become common enough practice – regression to childhood – since none could trespass into forbidden midnight alleys for a homebound shuffle. Though they wouldn't be as intense as this wake, as we would sink into slumber softly, lain out around beds, sofas, and improvised nests of sleeping bags and spare sheets and pillows. Those evenings had stunk less of desperation, but their cloistered resignation shared a common thread; meeting with friends, staying up despite a strict disapproving rule, resisting indolence. As limited room as my partner and I had for guests, we held small apartment concerts such as artists had done in the centuries preceding us – and when allies took initiative to organize also, so headed we into cramped apartments for shindigs. And these would last as long as we dared push them, would end in jam sessions, we would make noise, and then neighbours would knock on our walls, spooked at the idea of calling the police in these days. And we would calm down, happy that fear of authority muzzled noise complaints.

Though as opposed to tonight's hunger, in those homely soirees we would eat. Given that chances to go out on the town had become rare, those within our sphere populi would save their earnings (if earnings they still had), to splurge on domestic luxuries (AKA, grub... mostly).

And we'd have food delivered at our doors. Stores had become useless – their shelves were empty. At least by ordering in we could see what stores actually had in stock. Though perishable foods were scarce, there was abundance in hailing seitan, and soy-insect meats, and mushrooms, or soy-insect-mushroom pastes, or the likes, as well as cheese. The only bountiful fresh vegetables, for some reason, were onions. We would fry onions next to mealworm or grasshopper patties flavoured like turkey, beef or some other we never had tasted, or smoked (one patty of seitan and whichever bugs, had a flavour of smoked rosemary which made my mouth water), and then we'd melt grated cheese on top, serve the whole between slices of stale rye bread. The other simplest near-greens were either rutabaga or beans – and either refried beans or rutabaga french fries satisfied anyone. And if we had to eat the same every night, it wasn't the worst, even though from time to time a salad, or a nice stew, or anything that wasn't derived from grain or mushroom bug puree, flavoured or not, would have been refreshing.

Just like this night I missed being on stage with my bandmates, I had missed them this summer. The foreground of minuscule gatherings of peers was pleasant, but couldn't compare; apartment concerts as resistance sustenance prior to better things returning. With our band practices occurring infrequently, travel made difficult. And it's being together that's the best part. We get more creative, we get on the same page, when we are in the same place. Songwriting becomes instinctive, breakthroughs are spontaneous, work doesn't require the laborious concentration of one individual striving to shut out the outside world. When I worked alone, I sometimes missed the manual labour that had occupied my younger days. Before earning a living with music... my first job had been as a plasterer, then I did other small masonry. With those jobs, it was simple to concentrate – you get in, you see what you need to do, and you do it. The initial task is clearly visible, the end result is clearly visible. Back then some of my coworkers couldn't wrap their heads around a creative process, and song writing. Because you don't see what there is to do, you don't see the end result. You have to feel what the song is, and feel it when it's done. The coworkers who could understand, were those who for instance supervised work, or themselves designed elements in construction – things built in empty space, conceived within thin air. Of course their end result was visible, but there were similarities. In any case, it was nice to remember work that had a clear end result, and some sort of objective sense, not that I would have wanted to go back to it. The memory only evoked a tangibility I longed for.

Writing music with my bandmates had none of the tough-to-chew textures I dealt with when I was alone. Melodies came to me quite naturally. Grooves in my own style, in my own right. Lyrics were more difficult, perhaps (probably?) because I didn't sing. When I whistled I had perfect pitch, but my voice didn't know where notes were, and unless I whistled at each turn, I was unable to sing a melody to save my life. Sim wouldn't agree to too many instrumentals (though we needed some, for when he had to excuse himself from stage, as he did). Then I couldn't say why, but it was harder for Sim to paste lyrics onto tunes we had composed without him; then if he wrote the lyrics alone, he tried to put social context, engagement, and that kind of crap I had no inclination for, and other band members weren't keen on either. Or it ended up being very cliché. Sim needed us there to push him beyond the banal imagery we had been spoon fed since birth. Ivan or H. managed to get lyrics done too, but Sim got moody if we penned a song as a group yet without him – made him feel useless and left out, which was conceivable, reckoning he was the singer.

In contrast, working with K.L.U... The standoffish studio musicians, the competitive pop-producer directed environment, had nothing of the creative arts I thrived on, and for which I endeavoured in this vocation or mine – and those arts that created meaning in existence. In short... had nothing of the creative arts! It was mechanical, robotic bullshit labour at its pinnacle. A good group of weirdos was lacking in my new scenery. Though I couldn't complain. We did have some chums – not exactly a gang of weirdos, but an amiable cohort. I had extras contracts here and there. I did lose countless contracts in recent years when the ban on unmusic was lightened (on the basis of stock-purpose, of small productions, of allowing it where it quote-unquote wouldn't hurt the *creative economy*). That was when my lady and I, we had stopped watching the news altogether, I remember. That decades old ban (from before my time) – such as the bans on artificially created animation, and images, and writing – that had safeguarded creativity was slowly deregulated. And once trespassed beyond that threshold, what was the point of anything? If our breed couldn't articulate its inner needs – that is, to externalize: express, ecstasy, explore – in imaginary societies of alienation evermore embodying our sorry insignificance, fuck the news, fuck the apparatus, fuck it. If a person in your life is toxic, you stop talking to them. Unlimited strike, unlimited boycott. And I lost contracts, dealt with unemployment for stretches, each of us did, we stopped watching the news, we had apartment concerts and our mirth seeped out into the curfew flushed streets, carried off, echoing, certainly.

But this summer had been dry. That was one difference with that evening.

21

El. wiped under her eyes with her palms.

22

Promising to stay by the door, I couldn't help but admire the architecture around me. A city at night is a hauntingly magnificent place, palace, one I had never seen unlit. My eyes, familiarized with dim brilliance at this nocturnal hour, could conceive the straight lines, curved corners or moulded contours of nearby buildings, in the radiance of her majesty the moon. The vibrations registered by our feet had calmed down – not at a halt altogether, they were more audible, albeit less tremulous –, at that time when El. was becoming very anxious to hide anew. I pleaded so that my over-confident self could remain where we were, appreciating a fresh breath and the mild weather so.

The distinct thuds of detonations echoing on urban expanse spun around us, but I could still tell the direction they were coming from. I thought of fireworks. The only other time I had heard such sounds, it was when there had been fireworks.

23

When we swore we'd stop watching the news, we had a quiet bash, unworthy of anyone's attention, not even our own. We mocked events by our discretion. Candlelight across the apartment, hither and thither flames, soft yellow glimmer dancing. Guests moving to hush, open window gust-clamour, songs of silence. We played with orange peels – oranges near impossible to come by – squeezing them over open flame for gushing oils to spark. Many peels were already too dry, but the sparks that sprung forth had more beauty than fireworks. To our eyes, at least. With springs, and flints, powder that burned and things from our recycling jars, we improvised displays of shimmer that shone through incense smoke. Dancing with one another, our dances private, unspoken. Wicks wavering at our movements; shades quivering left and right behind our boogying, as it happened, surrounded by luminous blossoms. Surrounded by luminous blossoms, shadows left and right quivering, we played games – board games, gestures, storytelling, Werewolf, games with complicated rules, or simple games from childhood. Even friends from the capital came down, H., and Ivan. Sim thought we were silly, he didn't want to join in. That was some time ago now... Not each of us abided by our resolution, but I had neither news bulletins nor newspapers nor gossip payed attention to since.

Inserting itself within this sweet recollection – that image of the older lady asking a tweed-clad gentleman seated in front of me, in the humid, malodorous train car the previous evening. What pitiful human beings. Innocents, worrying for a world of their faults. Innocents, scared while ignoring the fact that they were the source of their fear. They had caused their torments. They would continue to cause their torments. They perpetuated lies. And they convinced themselves that their torments came by no faults of their own, by none of the lies they believed – those people had not once in their lives considered that their beliefs were wrong. I had, and then later, I gave up. When we stopped following the news – how laughable, their arguments to permit the use of unmusic, let us fall apart. As if creativity was not the single greatest adaptation factor for humankind. As if our survival did not depend on it.

Shadows moving with the curtains by the open-window breeze swaying. Steaming reflections of flames across our pale polished hardwood floor. Something about our apartment that night was like water. It was water, flames burned around; we were vapour in between. My girlfriend whispered in my ear that night, "I'm happy we're dropping out. What's the use otherwise, when no one cares?" That was it... "when no one genuinely cares." No one genuinely did care. Had there been a time... there had been a time, when uncreative generators had been banned – but that was before us – or when we had established boycotts, sat in recycle-circles dissecting tablet-phones, writing slogans on walls and banners. It fell apart – what venom had been injected into the bloodstream? Migraines had interrogated: were we giving up? But our band, we weren't, since our music would ring true. Perhaps our music was social after all... could there at any level be *arts for arts sake*, when the existence or art as humanity's heart had electronic guns aimed towards it? Our conclusion was we hadn't given up... I kept on believing that. Was I the only one, now? But we truly hadn't... We had celebrated by candlelight – hope was intimate. Hope is an intimate matter. Who went with fear, without hope, who perpetuated lies, what promise crumbled, what venom had been injected into the bloodstream? Humans are a predatory species, and having become top predator, nothing was left but for humans to hunt themselves.

Making a living as long as there is a living to be made... Ironic, that tragic events today lead to the cherished memory of that enchanting candlelight evening, sprouting our own miniature fireworks. Yet fondly remembered overcoming of hard times... hard times nonetheless...

24

We went back upstairs at a moment when windows were shaking through seismic shudders: rattling, up and down the street, applauded the belligerent presence.

In our hall, El. Excused herself; she wanted to be alone. Excitedly, I sat by K.. When I told her we had been outside, she giggled; she wasn't surprised. K.'s mind was wandering. She questioned whether I thought we should have a keyboard player in the band. I stated I thought we were too many as it was (and if El. Should join our ranks?), but that if we should add something, it should be a saxophone; "I don't see what good a keyboard would be when we already have two guitars and a bass." K. laughed because it wasn't the first time I brought up the idea of a saxophone player. I teased K., "what else are you thinking about?".

She sighed "I was wondering, if we had managed more success in the past, if we'd be in different circumstances."

- Oh come on, let's not brood about any of that shit. That's the one thing I hate.

- You hate all shit, I don't know which shit you're referring to. But you're right, everyone's in a mess... anyway... It's not like they open up the borders based on success... But... can you... I wonder... forget... why do you hate the news so much?

- The news?

- Politics?

- Why the hell shouldn't I?

- Well, it's... if we don't pay attention to it... I mean, being involved in it is what makes a difference, a little, you know? It's... that way everyone decides what we can do. I'm not dedicated to the idea, but...

-    Decide? You mean we all vote, and that way we decide what we want? Like that works. Who decides what? What is there to decide? Vote – 49% one way, 51% another way... and case closed? 49% too bad, so sad, deal with it? Or if only 10% of a population votes, that's what we get... but it's democracy! How rich... What is there to decide... You get up in the morning, and try to do something that day. You do your own thing. Other people, you just try to work with them. That's all there is to it.

-    But...

-    *Fuck sakes*, K., if you want to talk about that sort of thing, I'll go sit with Ivan. He knows why I hate that shit; he's had enough, him too.

"I just wanted to know..." she whispered while I got up. Before I walked away though, she grabbed my hand – bizarre, as K. was a solitary type, who stayed in her bubble, and not the kind of person who takes any physical contact lightly; with K., any physical gesture, any touch, had a strong meaning. At a loss, she peered me in the eyes and uttered as some sort of hymn "Do you think we'll ever make it?"

– Sure we will, I blankly asserted.

– How do you know?

–   Sometimes... out there, I hear a tune bad, so horribly bad, but that people say they like. They say they like it, even though it clearly has no musical value... I get to thinking *There's no way that what I play is worse than this... and people say they like this, so there's gotta be some people who'll like my music.* That's how I know. It's logical. To me it is, anyways. That's how I know we'll make it. If not with this album, then with the next, or though a chance meeting, or a gig... I don't think anyone really gets anywhere by hard work alone; we'll find the luck we need somewhere, some day or another. And until we find luck or luck finds us, we'll keep on compensating with hard work. But the loads of people with bad taste, that can't be all there is. There's got to be good people, with good taste. Because hell, we're not so unique.

–   I didn't mean our music, she chuckled, her brilliant eyes projecting starlight, but I like what you said. I feel good about our music too. As long as we like what we play, I think we've made it.

–   It's easy for you to feel confident, you're the biggest virtuoso this side of the planet. You put classical musicians to shame.

–   Playing alone... she sighed, releasing my hand; it can be refreshing, but it has nothing on playing with a band, her eyes turning to embers from the respawned heat of her personality, the same energetic heat she had on stage, when she soared, used every bit of material to burn down the venue.

–   You know that pop singer I play for? She gets high alone. Her other musicians, they all get high alone...

–   Why would they do that?

–   Exactly. And they don't really talk. And they don't record like we do, playing all at the same time. They do their individual takes; they don't share anything with each other. I barely know them. We practice together on occasion, but you feel like a session musician... or, we are... We play for her, but she doesn't have a backing band. I get in a bit of creative input because I want to, but the others... When they come, some of them are stoned. You don't really know because they don't talk anyways. There's no passing-around-of-the-joint, no bong-circle. There's no wine bottle after a recording is done. Plus, she works with one of those mixing-mixing-over-mixing studios where you don't even know when you're all done recording, because you won't listen to a rough mix together. They just tell you to go home, and you'll hear the song when you'll hear the song. Most of them don't even take any sort of social drug. They are more the opium, or even heroine type. I know the singer, she takes this weird thing called *Mathylocassadrine*. She gets these weird packs smuggled from those countries where it's legal. The packs have a really Art Nouveau label, look like something copying Mucha or Klimt. Yea... she told me... because sometimes she emanated a super strong smell of frankincense, and she told me something like "the Solomon Brothers' stuff" was Frankincense scented. Apparently you just mix it in with a little bit of hot bath water, and you get high. Doesn't sound that fun to me. Alone in the tub and no place to go.

–   I think that's sad.

–   That is sad... but then, she pays me (or her label does). And I enjoy the feeling that thanks to my input, her otherwise... what word to use... derivative... or un-noteworthy music becomes worthwhile.

–   I prefer making guitars. I wouldn't want to play with that sort of musicians, K. spat out despisingly.

–   That explains why you don't take up anyone on their invitations. Because you must get loads of them...

–   Too many. Hey, tell me something interesting; what guitar does her guitarist use?

–   Ah, I can actually answer that for you. You'd be interested, but he's not too friendly – I tried chatting with him. It wasn't like he'd be worth knowing. For a couple of warmer-sounding tunes he uses an old Krunk Ani. For others, he uses a Backlund 100 model, which to be honest, I think looks really cool, but sounds boring. A bit like a St-Vincent guitar; it looks very nice, and different, but the tones are dull, unless you plan on playing only funk or bland pop, or overloaded with effects. I guess they're for overloading – they retain clarity well. Maybe if you play prog? A St-Vincent is the better of the two. He also brought a Steinberger a couple of times.

–   Well, at least he's got that going for him.

–   What do you mean?

–   Come on, Steinbergers? Those guitars are so ugly... only someone who really likes the sound, and feel of the guitar, can play one of those. They sound decent...

–   Well, that about covers it.

–   You know, I was serious about making you a new bass. It would change your whole game to have an instrument with more sustain.

–   I have instruments with more sustain, I just don't need it that much. My playing style, you know. Think of classic Hofner basses, they don't have sustain either, but that's what people look for.

–   You know that I could put in a mute? Or, a kind of mute. I could easily make it so that you could switch from having sustain to having no sustain. Unrelated, I was thinking about something I wanted to try out; maybe I could try it out on your bass.

–   What was it?

–   Frets that you screw in. I will need minuscule screws; two very thin, and very long, and two more, less long. Hear me out before thinking I'm completely insane. I'm just so tired of there being so few guitar innovations nowadays, you know? Everyone is just rehashing the same ideas. Even I'm rehashing. Some of the last guitars I made, I put in a tuning-fork bridge. Even in a solid-body, I made a small chamber for the tuning-fork bridge. We're all hacks. But, I hatched a few new ideas, and one of them was the screw-in frets. One of the reasons was that sometimes you love a guitar, but the frets don't do it for you. Their size – ultra-wide, medium-jumbo, tall, short, etcetera – or their material. I think nickel sounds noticeably better, some people really prefer steel, then brass has got its fans, and *evo*. And the brass fans have to get re-fretted because so few electrics are sold with brass. Flat crown, round crown, and so on. I thought there could be a better way, and a way to put in frets that might even sound better, since it's directly on the fret that the string vibrates.

I've been working on this project. You take the guitar neck. You have your truss rod in the middle, then on each side you put two rods, like stiffening rods. So far, nothing new. The thing is, they won't be *only* stiffening rods; they'll be hollow. What I want is for them to amplify the sound. These two rods are hollow, and made to resonate. The long screws, you screw in to hold in the frets, through the fretboard, into these rods, so that the screws actually conduct the sound which then gets amplified by the rod. Or, they'll add acoustic quality, better tone. Then, the shorter screws go on each side of the truss rod (but they should be too short to actually go too deep into the neck. Because the neck has to take the sound, you know). You'd need a neck that's thick enough though. I've been saving up, because of course, it means I need a machine to make the right-size screw holes into fret-wire, and then I need the custom size screws to go with the resonating rods, which I need to manufacture. And the screws must be strong, but ridiculously small, if we want to put in small or narrow-tall frets... How's about it? I could also put in another idea – an easily changeable nut. They've been making nuts with screws for adjustable height. I've been thinking about nuts with screws, so that a person can have different nuts, if the player wants to change string gauges, or... maybe it's all excessive.

–   Sounds good K., but I just play bass, I'm not crazy like you.

–   Isn't it a great idea though?

–   I guess! But, a lot of guitars never even go through a re-fret... Maybe if it makes the instrument sound better?

–   That's what I was thinking! She whooped, a wide smile on her face that sadly faded fast, as she had to admit; if industry comes back to normal... and we can start ordering parts again... and, god forbid, custom parts...

–   K.? Can you tell me a joke? I miss your humour, I asked, since I realized she had barely made a funny comment all night, though I hadn't been by her side for most of it.

25

Ivan inhaled slowly and deeply, and held in the smoke before exhaling as silence entombed us. We discussed confusion, how confusion is a form of paralysis. Ivan was rambling "I feel confused, I do, and confusion really is, that I can't move forward. Of course I can't go backwards. Only amnesia would mean going backwards. That's not true. There are some people strong enough to convince themselves that events or facts aren't true. Strong – I said strong. I don't know for certain. It seems to me that only a very strong mind could deny reality – deny everything that its senses are telling it, and decides to believe something of its own invention. Then again, maybe that depicts a mind that is weak. It would refuse to recognize what it perceives. It doesn't refuse to perceive things – it simply doesn't perceive past its own invention. That would mean that creativity is inherent to everyone, but only strong minds can shut it out. Hmm. I don't think that's right. Some aren't creative at all, even as children. Maybe, only stronger minds yet can both shut it out, and tap into it, at will. Some kids lose their creativity in school, but many of very educated people are highly creative. We praise the creativity of small children, because their imagination is in full bloom, but much of what they come up with is crap. Like a room made of pizza, or clothes that absorb all the filth from yourself so you never have to shower. A room made of pizza would be horrible, and would have to be eaten or it would rot – in other words, it's just a fucking huge pizza. A shower isn't only to get clean – you can clean yourself with wipes and so on, there are many ways to clean oneself – showers, baths, they relax muscles, relieve tension... go without a shower for a while to see how appeasing they are. Though, okay, such clothes would be nice to some extent. Kids have imagination, but it's unfocused, untrained, unpractical. No, I must have been wrong – it is weak people who can shut out reality, because they don't have the strength to see reality, much less cope with it."

I slipped in "Unless you really don't care", but he didn't pay attention to me. He kept on going "So if you are weak, you can prevent yourself from going forward, and if you are very weak, or have amnesia, or brain damage, you can perhaps go backwards, but no one sane or safe can go backwards, that's impossible. But, you can stay stuck. You can stay in the same place, indefinitely, painfully, and that is confusion. When you are confused, your comprehension stops, your free-flowing thought stops, your clear perception stops. When you are doing mathematics, and you are confused, you cannot finish your calculations. When you are learning and become confused, you cannot keep on learning, you don't understand. When you are reading and become confused, you cannot keep on reading – words don't have meaning, sentences become blank spaces. You have to free yourself from confusion, rid yourself of it. Take a break, breath, read the sentence over, start the problem from the beginning, try to figure out what's confusing you."

I asked Ivan "Do you regret not having pursued studies in university?" He stared at me unblinkingly, his thick horseshoe moustache crowning over his straight-lined mouth. He asked "Was there ever something else you wanted to do, before you dedicated yourself to music?" I peered at the ground. There must have been something, though it was so far away. When I was a little boy, I had toys of construction vehicles, and building materials. I used to play *construction yard*, draw out structures, pretending we (my crew and I) should build them. I thought, when I was really little, I would have wanted to work in construction, and mostly, to operate heavy machinery. I had remained interested in everything technical. When I was about ten, I helped my grandparents repair an old mechanical pocket watch. They said it wouldn't have been worth the cost to go to the watchmakers. It was a worthless old timepiece. They didn't really need it; it was a game between me and them, to repair the antique. Maybe at one point after that, I had been interested in watchmaking. I also liked to draw, but that was another matter. All kids like to draw. Thinking, Ivan's speech, it was making me a little confused as well. I didn't want to think about it anymore. I was a musician, what did it matter what else there was to do in the world? I wasn't going to do it. I would play music, and others would let me play music. "A watchmaker", I decided, unflinchingly; "Who would make real, mechanical watches. Nothing with batteries, nothing that wouldn't last. Real, immortal, mechanical watches." Ivan laughed "Immortal... wouldn't even have to be greased or maintained." He paused, took a couple of tokes, and confessed (for himself?) " I know I should have done more." I sought to comfort him, stating he did plenty for the band – worked on our original songs penned songs, played flawlessly... He interrupted me: "No, outside... outside of the band. I should have done more." I asked him "what, you're supposed to work two to three jobs? Come on man, you're single, you're still doing fine, no?" He smirked, "you know what I mean. We're locked in here. We are confused. Okay, we're not locked in, but we can't go forward. We are confused..." half laughing; "that's 'cause we didn't look at the problem. Take it from the top. And if I try to not be confused... I go back, I look at the problem... Here I am..."

"Hey man, that's not our problem", I exclaimed. But he just puffed and nodded sideways. "Well, we're in the problem. If it's not our problem, I don't know what our problem is. Lack of food? I'm pretty damn hungry... You know, I used to think we could make a difference, but people are just so damned stupid. Maybe I'm just on a sad buzz." I agreed with him; "exactly, man, do yourself." "Oh, I've done myself", he asserted, "I haven't done myself in yet, but I've done myself." I stopped him: "No, I meant you do you."

He replied "I know what you meant. That's all you ever mean. No offence man, I love you, man. You're a brother. You're my brother. You're a brother to me. I've looked up to you maybe a little too much. I like your attitude. Not caring. I was sick of caring. When you care about people, they become defensive little bitches. My dad was a real bitch that way. Every time I give him advice, he'd get so defensive, you couldn't say anything to him anymore. Then again, my mom was a bit the same. Not a hundred percent though. She'd lock up, be passive-aggressive, and act like you don't matter. He'd argue with you about who-the-hell knows what, to try to make you unsay what you said, or try to look smarter or something. At one point, I just let him make his mistakes alone. I stopped seeing them. I lived my own life, in my own succession of crummy apartments, and enjoyed myself. People say kids are difficult. You put a hat on them, they cry, throw the hat. Don't want to eat, throw food, cry when you dress them, cry when you put them to bed. They don't want to be potty trained, they push away their potty, don't want to be on the toilet, they piss of the floor, crap in the bathtub... But then adults are just the same. They don't want to be helped, corrected, put in their place. They don't want their safety zone – their diaper – taken away from them, even if it's full of shit, even if they're shitting themselves. What do you want to tell someone who gets upset because you want to help them stop shitting themselves? Say 'listen, you're spending outside your means. Do you want help with a budget' or 'cut your goddamned credit cards, they're no good they are', or 'looks like you're getting a drinking problem', or 'you shouldn't vote for that party, it's a bunch of propagandist bullshit'... People don't want any of that. As soon as you comment, as a friend, as a fellow human, as soon as you try to start a calm, rational discussion, they pull out their knives. Yea, I gave up on all that stuff, and I thought you were so... so fucking cool, so fresh, and ahead of everyone else for having given up. For saying 'fuck it. Let them help themselves'. I thought you were right. That we can't help them if they don't help themselves. Like what they say in psychology. You know, if they don't want to make changes themselves, that no amount of therapy, of treatment, of information, of well-rounded arguments, of philosophy, would change them, or change their minds. Free market, random choice, decision fatigue, dictatorship of the *consumariat*. I thought I wanted to be more like you. Let myself go forward even if society stayed back, as backwards as it was... is. I wanted to play music, to do only that, to be unbothered. We shared this, you inspired me, man. I gave up on arguing, I never argued anymore. I stopped talking, left, ignored people, ignored the news... I barely knew what was going on until I learned we couldn't freely travel anymore... and only because Sim informed me, because I wanted to see where we could tour. Now it looks like we can't plan in advance no matter how advanced we are ourselves. We can't plan anything, can't do anything, because all that surrounds us, is clamped at our ankles like a ball and chain. Slowing us down... or is it slowing us down? I was thinking about how we ignored what went on in the world, how we let it go on around us, without a bother. It was pleasant... no fussy bastards taking offence in not being right all the time, or protecting their mistakes. Sitting in their shit-overflowing diapers. But how can they change only by themselves? Even when someone in therapy *can only change if they want to*, they need that stimulus. Nothing can happen without stimulus. We can't expect anything to change if we don't prompt that change. I thought I could let actuality solve itself without taking action. But actuality is action. Inaction doesn't make actuality – it would make *inactuality* if it should make anything. Inaction is stagnation – it is confusion that does not know what to do in the world. It does not move. It stays stagnant. It cannot or does not want to comprehend the problem. Sometimes, we are confused because we do not want to understand, to put in the brain power to actually understand. Some action may look like inaction, while being action. Non-violent protesters, having a sit-in, or chaining themselves to trees, seem inactive, but in reality, if their actions are made visible, if they are deliberate, made public, and have a goal, then they are actions. They are not *inactions* because they are discrete, or calm. Inaction goes with a specific desire *not to do*, or *not to take part in something*. It does not have goals, or goals outside of the preservation of its own inactivity. One's inaction can only become part of actuality through the actions of others – as of such, it is not the inaction of one that is actual, it is the action of others, though maybe inspired by inaction. If inaction is confusion, the *inactive*, the idle, are confused. The active would act should there be the inactive or not, because they are not confused.

They are moving, they are active, they take action. Can one become confused, though, by being with those who already are? The inactive, I mean... If inactivity should overtake activity, there should be no more actuality. The world would stagnate in confusion. But then, we could say that the adults who don't better themselves and insist on repeating their mistakes are active... since they pursue their mad endeavors... but it's their activity that fucks everything up. What to do then? I'm back to square one. Is the only truly worth-while action, action not turned towards the world, but the self? That can't be it... How would our lives look if we all were inactive? How would we all proceed? Take part in organization, in making the wheels turn, getting things done... transporting food, building shelters, what do I know..? You're right perhaps that it wasn't our problem, but, it became our problem, we are in the problem. We are here, confused... Or maybe not... we did our part by avoiding this nonsense, and if others had done the same... that would have been our action. We would have shared messages of sensibility and intelligence. Through our music, our celebration of human spirit. Things to last. And lead our lifestyles in the trend of our boycott-generation, inhabiting simple housing, or voluntarily sub-par residences, in protest of standardized aesthetics, and gentrification. But did we exhibit this message, our culture, these ideas? I honestly don't believe did. None of us have any idea what to do. We don't know what we're doing. And if we do get blown to bits... We're confused, and *inactual*. Now I'm just thinking I shouldn't have interrupted my studies. I should've found a way to play music – that is what I desire – but I should have done something more. Maybe there would have been something I could have done to make things better."

"But... for instance, your songs make the world better; maybe you couldn't have written them if you did it differently. You remember your tracks on the soundtrack of *The great audience embargo?*", I tried to reassure him. But he was lucid, and after a few puffs, he spoke "Maybe I would've, maybe I wouldn't've. Maybe I would have written better songs, maybe not. It's impossible to say, and it's useless to speculate.

But I have to say, if we make it through whatever is going on, I want to make more of a difference. Go figure how."

I had a pressing feeling, like my best friend was breaking up with me. But we weren't a couple, we were bandmates and buddies, we had a right to disagree on stuff as long as we weren't assholes about it. I could think of activism as bleak and useless, and he could think my blank votes and boycott of the news were – how did he phrase it? – confusion, but if we didn't preach to each other, it would be fine. And even then, he hadn't talked about activism. And maybe he wasn't as lucid as I had believed. Earlier that day, in the radio station, and in this very hall, we had both mocked what comprises "actuality". A sudden epiphany? More like Ivan was the drunk who swore he'd never drink again. And if he would drink less, if he did become more "aware", "awoken", he would never be some militant partisan, always sober. Hadn't we, just some hours ago, sneered at Sim's being concerned? Was I learning that dope affected Ivan more than I believed, or in fact had I always known it? It could be that we both realized new things about each other, or that we realized nothing new; we were parodying each other in a sleepless stupor, and it was laughable. His philosophishing about confusion and activity would leave as much of an impression on us the next morning, as to raise an eyebrow, and giggle "what?"

I felt cold though, perhaps because we had been joyfully united by our refusal of the supposed obligations that society tried its best to force upon us, or refusal of sordid morality. Or I felt cold from intruders at my core that I could neither identify nor fathom. Invasive species despite themselves changing, perhaps devastating their ecosystem; species that are invasive do not see themselves as such, they simply lead their lives. Invasive feelings... One more change, when it was already tough brushing away further uncertainties. I had to ask Ivan, in the end, "So what are we now?", and Ivan answered nonchalantly "I love you, man! You're my brother!" He handed me the joint, which I readily accepted. It wasn't the time to sober up.

26

Sim called our attention to view outdoors. We flocked to him from all corners of the hall. I had taken more ecstasy, and felt a wave of bliss washing over my entire being (oh boy, fused with lingering shrooms...). At Sim's side: he pointed upwards, to the building in front of ours. One of the high windows – light was lambent behind it. It was obvious that it wasn't one of the ceiling lights, that the power hadn't come back, by how dim it was, and by the way it flickered, or moved. It must have been a flashlight, that was our guess. Who could it be, we wondered. Was it the military, inspecting the buildings? Rioters who were hidden, or had hidden... what? Were they ordinary people (admitted to or intruding in the broken safety perimeter), roaming these infinitely large, vacated buildings? Were they just like us? We noticed also, that the sky was getting clearer.

The colour of the sky brought me back to that time we played in the famous week-over-night festival; nonstop for a whole week, on three stages, in the dead of summer, in a valley buried in the Carpathian range. A week during which every band would play more than once, a week to drain you, a week to replenish you. Jams, energy, seeing shows yourself. Taxing as some aspects were, the festival meant great fun for musicians. You'd really get to connect with colleague-bands, to invite new musician friends onstage, to free-flow, during your 3rd or 4th set of the week. 4 sets was what we had gotten – once during the day, two in the dead of night, and one during an evening. We were only there for the last few days, and our last set was in the wee hours of the penultimate twilight. The sky had donned that dark blue hue, misleading one for a lighter shade as it was the first colour to break prolonged blackness. The considerably chillier night air was damp enough to wring out. It really affected me, how beautiful a clear-sky cloud-free morning it would be, where the chirping of birds would consort the lush taste of adventure, while we were playing the slow, nostalgic (with a heroic touch to it, or that's what we want people to feel in it, anyways), two-beat rhythm of *The ballad of Harry McClintock*. Fortunately we recorded that set, because we played it with three members of another band, a band from Western Europe called *Lueg mol*. In that band there was one girl who sang and played clarinet. She didn't play clarinet on that song; she had enough instinct to know it didn't fit the feel. She did the most heavenly country-gospel harmonies, soaring somewhere in the mountain air... It most probably was one of the best shows we ever did, and we later wanted to release it as an album – which the guests were okay with as long as their names were mentioned on the album sleeve (naturally! We would have painted the scene in our liner notes!), but for contractual reasons (their uncooperative record label), we couldn't until a few years would have passed. It was still sitting in our stock of unused material, b-takes, potential b-sides... things we didn't know how to use, or where to use, or kept for the right occasion, or couldn't use yet, but didn't want to throw out.

The hum of our panting in the large hall, the flickering lamplight in a window of the neighbouring tower... I imagined "the sky has that same colour", and then laughed at myself "it's been, what, two years? And you think you can recall the right shade?", then I shrugged "maybe I can. Maybe I can remember that distinct a shade. Maybe that moment was special enough."

Except for Ivan, my fellows urged I stop laughing, in the time they milled over who it could be, up there, in our vicinity (mulling over something we can't know, can't figure out, and can't interact with). Were we in danger? Were the buildings being searched? Or was it something else? Sim suggested "I think it's ordinary people. The military, they've got various equipment and techniques. They wouldn't be fuddling around with high-beam flashlights. That's amateur stuff. People who'd want ill would watch out too... no, that has to be ordinary folks; what do you guys think?"

That got me considering "Hey but, if people can move around, doesn't that mean <u>we</u> can move around?"

–   That depends, maybe they were stuck in there before too, Ivan supposed.

–   Maybe they're with those people who hang around in the sewers, or access tunnels, and all that junk, who know how to move about, K. surmised.

–   Are there really people like that? squealed Sim.

–   Sure there are.

–   Can we get to know people like that?

–   I just want to lie down on my fucking bed, yawned H.

–   I wish we had power, and the sludge, I prompted.

The sludge was the name we gave to extra-strong, heavy, thick, and truly disgusting coffee-type brew we drank upon necessity to keep us wide awake. Usually we would have cakes, cookies, or milk chocolate, or white chocolate – candy wouldn't cut it (too thin or volatile a flavour) – to balance out the mouth curdling bitterness. After keeping the pot hot, warmed up, hot again, the aggressively acrid aroma would get more burned than smoky. Ivan couldn't drink it on an empty stomach – it had caused him to wretch now and again. Sim had a tendency to abuse *the sludge*, in some addicted, adrenaline freak, hype, sadomaso enthusiastically yelling out "the sludge!" and refilling our cups. He loved to be intense, and loved to be hyper. His feelings were always absolute, never had much nuance. He couldn't say "I like this, but it's a bit annoying." If he liked it, he liked it, and if it were to be annoying, it'd be annoying. If he was hyper, he became completely hyper. For this reason we closely monitored his drug intake, and aimed to keep him more sober than the rest of us. The only drug we let him abuse was *the sludge*, and that's because it gave him the runs. Needless to say, he would quit the stuff himself. It wouldn't give him the runs straight away.

It would take a few days. He'd have to chug-a-lug-lug his gallons, but he'd get there; his behind would spurt out oil spills as tar-thick as what we drank. We didn't fear he'd suffer Montezuma's revenge during concerts, because we could more-or-less predict and plan around the incident. We'd remain attentive for when he would leap off-stage with wide, panic-stricken eyes, and we would break out into a prolonged jam. H. liked to keep track of how long this jam would go on, and at this point in time, our record stood at a whopping 23 minutes and a half. Thinking about it, between Ivan needing regular piss-breaks and Sim exploding from the rear mid-gig, we were a very considerate group – in addition to H., K. and I having the moxie of a power trio.

Glory I loved some of those jams. I can offer no explanation as to why countless individuals were bereaved of the ability to lose themselves in pure sound. I spit on people who only trust in music they (think they) can dance to. My theory is that those people never actually listen. If they have their dance tracks in the background, it's out of fear of emptiness. But they don't listen to their crap. They might know the words to impose feelings within themselves. As in, they don't reach for the feeling in the music; they let lyrics dictate how the music is supposed to make them feel. They can't stand songs in languages they don't understand, because those lyrics can't tell them how to feel (consciously). I think each music schoolroom class, for kids, should have *drone* sessions. Drones in traditional musics, in heavy metal, nuances of drones, to exercise each child's acuteness to introspection.

And so, what if those jams left us – we were told by bad producers, and so-called *professionals* from the music industry – as having only an artistic, musically literate, and more *selective* following with "limited commercial potential". The likes had been said about bands that went very far too. Bands from a hundred years ago, or more, from the golden age of rock music. Probably executives had asked early rockers why they'd rather play "selective *music*", as opposed to more popular *country*... But how could we trade in? People who listened to our music needed our music. And our music had to reach more people, simply because our music is better. We know that. We won't stop believing that. Don't ask me how individuals could elect political death-cults, reemerging racists, and sexists, and capitalists, but couldn't understand purpose. Humans are a predatory species... WE, we are the ones beyond, we are the ones who have understood more – artistic endeavour, is the endeavor to further our kind's consciousness and instincts.

We need to play that music. On those stages – under lights, before a range, a realm of vague circular forms, stretching out, be the stages indoors where the realm was bound by suddenly rising walls, or outside, where width was limitless – I stopped existing. We all stopped existing, outside of our instinctive fingers, natural rhythmic impulses, and of the magnanimous sounds we produced. Never otherwise could we have magnified so, our presence, and the universe, how it impacted on us. I loved it when Sim got the runs from drinking too much *sludge*, since it left us with no alternative than to embrace our almost spiritual communion. Sim forced us to take up arms against the short-song, and pre-practiced solos only, pop music industry, that disdained every out-of-tune note as if they were de facto *bad*, and focused on image. Yea, image was there but... didn't anyone care what they were listening to? It seemed like the music industry was the biggest *plastic arts* domain as of yet.

Maybe it was those prolonged jams, in the end, that kept K. with us. She played superbly. So *articulate*, with such mastery over her entire fretboard. I was on occasion surprised she never went fretless, for more freedom. "Sustain" she repeated, "frets give sustain"; her new instrument had those movable frets.

The first time we met, K. and I, was at a jam. We were the only two who wanted to keep going after 6-7 minutes. For Joe Blows and Plain Janes, 6-7 minutes seemed like an eternity. Yet, in most every genre, on countless great albums, weren't there seemingly ever-flowing tunes? At this first encounter, she was brandishing a sexy offset body

Marrakesh guitar – which had extra frets in specific places in order to play maqamat – North African quarter tone scales. (For the anecdote, a year later, she unbolted the neck off of that guitar, and put it on an orange teardrop shaped guitar, just for pizzazz). We were young at that time, and she was only getting into researching, rethinking, and modelling alternative designs, or ideas, to put on her instruments. I recalled her stating in that period "I can't find a *different* guitar. Of course I can find tons of *good* guitars, but there are good guitars everywhere. And a good guitar player can get good sounds out of even bad guitars. Brand-name, non-brand-name, vintage, new, there are good guitars of all sorts. I'm tired of all the single-cut, double cut, s-style, t-style signature guitars out there... what's the point? The'll be forgotten as soon as they come out. There are hundreds of thousands of *good* guitars out there; give me something different", or something along those lines. She hunted rarities and oddities such as Alembics, Goya Rangemasters, Wurlitzer Geminis, or sliding pickup prototype guitars, or even an interesting (though for actual performers, pretty useless) Casio EG-5. Through the instruments I was into, I found an old Borisov Formanta, and I convinced buddies to chip in, a gift for her birthday. K. was – and this was perceptible at first sight – the kind of person you want to strive to make happy, because when you make them happy, they really radiate. They don't just thank you out of being polite, or as a due, their fleeting materialistic impulses washed over by a realization of disregard; they thank you through sincere appreciation of either present or gesture (not that being thanked should motivate any kind gesture; the point is, when she was happy, you could tell, and that made you happy). Unlike Ivan, who is the type of friend with whom you can complain, act pissed off, roam the streets (back when one could still roam the streets), with a frown on your face, K. is the friend who brings about cheer and good mood. And cheer and good mood were the sentiments shared at that first vamp, when we both kept on going while even the drum circle was aching to take a break. Maybe then, already, it was clear that we were meant to be bandmates.

I approached "K., d'you wanna fuckin' jam or something?"

—   Wait, so what are we doing? Yawned H.

—   Why would you want power, Sim commented irrelevantly.

—   You know, I'm just... (something was boiling up within me which even I hadn't foreseen early on); I'm fed up, dammit. We didn't do anything wrong; we want to have our show. You know what? This place, this is our fucking concert venue. You remember the old days when we'd have concerts any-fucking-where? Half-unplugged concerts in apartments, or entirely unplugged concerts? Just in normal peoples' apartments, in the living room. Ticket sales? At some point you just say "forget ticket sales". Free. You know? You just play. They'd have concerts in parks, in the street... on rooftops! But for our kind of situation where it has to be on the low-down, we could do it here. Look! It's big! People know how to get around. We'd have them sit down, you know? We'd do a long, drawn-out, meditative, sit-down set. All we need is to get the word around fast. I think, all we need is to get a power generator. No one'll see that coming: a whole concert. A power generator, cause we've got a drum set, we ain't gonna have Sim here ripping his throat out either. And if we don't do it here, we move our stuff, find somebody's garage! Or some open spot in the sewer systems! Let's do it!

I was appalled by the non-enthusiasm with which my proposal was met. "We don't even know if we'll get to leave this place alive, and how tomorrow will greet us" blurted Sim. "Really, what's the point of going out of our way just to play in front of *any* crowd?" H. Whined.

—   What the hell is wrong with you two? The point of playing in front of any crowd? When did it ever have a point, then? The point is playing! Sharing an experience! That's the point! It's its own point. That's what we do, that's all. And if we should be alive this morning? Who the fuck knows. But when's a better time? When should we play music, have a concert, if not at a time when there is nothing else? This is all we ever had, and all that we have left. As far as we know. Maybe the sun will rise, and we'll get to stroll out, like on a warm summer day. Maybe we'll get shot before we even step outside – don't ask me why. But no time like the present. This is the time where what we do has the most meaning. Because what we do is the only thing that still has meaning. Safety? Livelihoods? Enjoyment? Freedom? Ease? Prospects? That's gone. We're only left with our vocation, and everything it represents.

They stood in silence, looking down at their shoes, except for Ivan who broke the silence, stating "I wonder who that is up there, though."

27

I couldn't believe we had barely jammed in this night unabridged, K. and I (her and I, more so than with others). Yet before the sun-risen new chapter should have exhorted us towards obligations hazy in our vague-awareness of capacities and incapacities within reach, we did indulge in merciful ad-lib.

Her archtop didn't have too much volume unplugged, which wasn't an issue given it was also the case for my Hebros. H. had a tambourine; she pranced around keeping a beat. Sim was dozing again; Ivan had gone walking around the building; El. was sitting near us. It was getting considerably lighter out, and I was dreaming of hot oatmeal, with cold milk and raspberry jam. Rocking out helped me *unfeel* my hunger.

28

–   Aren't you concerned about your lady? K. murmured.

–   I'm thinking of her. I'm trying not to be concerned about anything, I acknowledged honestly.

The sun was getting lighter and lighter – from embryonic opaque saffron towards the translucent sand in the Elysium hourglass. I stood close to the windows to witness the gradual change, and to witness the fluttering veil-thin clouds gliding by, in the morning rays.

–   Well, where she is, it's farther from the border and the capital. That's something, K. tempted reassuringly.

–   Depends which border. And I really don't care. I went over the line today because I was scared. I just don't know if I can manage to tell her, because I'm a wimp and El. will still play with us sometimes, or always. I know she'll be forgiving if I tell her – likely she saw it betiding; Ivan joked about it, thought it was true –, but she'll also be stressed about future encounters, I explained, without mention of feelings, or was I most afraid? Adding; she's not jealous as long as it's sexual, but if it's emotional... logically she can be fearful.

–   She was already unnerved, K. bluntly confirmed; at the same time, I'm not aware... if that's what she likes. Everyone could see *you two* were attracted to each other by the way you both became pale and untalkative – or too talkative – when you were around each other. You get flushed around her.

–   Do I get flushed, or do I turn pale? I demanded, bothered by the conspicuous matter she brought at hand.

–   Depends where on your face. And I haven't looked at the rest of you, she giggled.

–   Is that a bad joke?

–   I was making a penis joke. I've never seen your penis. Neither will you see mine.

–   I wouldn't want to see yours even if you had one.

–   Come on, can't you pretend I have a penis, at least for the joke's sake? K. whined, before we both appreciated momentary tranquility, leading her to ask: so, you think you'll be able to go back?

–   Sure, why wouldn't I? I asked, knowing precisely what she was referring to, for even if I did try my best at not obsessing over what had arisen during the night, and if it were possible to take the train, or a bus, or anything, it was pestering my psyche, getting me into the worst of moods, since the E's effects were dissipating, and I hadn't taken anything else. But I also wanted to return, if it should prove possible.

–   *Balls' sakes* man, chances are we're... or in the midsts of... *Balls' sakes* – she threw her arms up – there might not even be a road anymore! She whispered harshly.

–   Sure there's a road, and there's a railway too. I came that way. Why wouldn't there be a railway?

–   Listen, I'm explaining... – she trailed off, shaking her head – are you going to crash with Ivan, or what?

–   I know what you're saying, and right now I don't know shit; what do you want me to say? It's okay not to know shit. It's all bullcrap. Fuck, can I take some mescaline, do you think? I could use some thick think-trip that'd last a good ten hours.

–   Man, you've had enough – or we've all had too much. And I think that if we have to negotiate with roadblocks, and tanks, with your neigh-saying high ass, Sim will have a heart attack, and we'll have to abandon you there.

–   Oh, you'd never find a better bass player these days.

–   You're right! She grinned; though... these days, doesn't look like we're going to need a bass player.

–   Dammit, yes we will! We're going to play! Here, or H.'s basement, or anywhere! We have to play somewhere, we have to let life happen. No, rather: we have to force life. Act to constraint life's persistence.

–   You know... this room is nice, but out there the streets are grey and filthy. People are scared shitless; they won't venture out to a concert. The ones who would have now reconsider. They won't do anything. Most people care about what goes on around them...

–   Hey, I care.

–   Yea, you do, but... you care a little differently than most people.

–   I have no idea what that means. Tell me something interesting instead. What are you thinking 'bout?

–   It'd bore you. I'm wondering what's... ensuing. It's a rather normal thing to wonder at present. But I'm also happy I have no one to worry about. No attachments, I can look out for myself, and that's that. And my instruments of course. And if my workshop could come out intact, that would be enjoyable... I have a few thousands worth of wood in there. At least if armies start pillaging, it's improbable they're gonna steal wood... or hell, those barbarians would be able to burn pristine heartwood come winter. If they do... I'm not sure what's worse to me. Maybe I'd rather it be stolen than reduced to ashes. Usage is usage... Maybe it'd be appreciated as firewood. As long as it doesn't smoulder under heaps of rubble...

29

    The day was upon us, and Sim had gone into a frenzy. Mad, he was wailing "Com-tee-ma-teh-lah! Com-tee-ma-teh-lah!" We gawked at him, tried to make sense of it. "Come to matela? Come thee my tailor? Committee mate... la?"; we couldn't make sense of any phonetic meaning discerned from his yell-of-a-chant. We could only assume that those sounds directly embodied his feelings, and went along with it. We held harmonies in the background, different notes changing notes, pretty accompaniments. Chanting, meditation – trance, chiming, communion, kinship, celebration, harmony, harmony, harmony (chromatic, reinventing it where we had cringed at disharmony; we create harmony anew), our chorus, our choir, our *coeur*, our hearts, we joined in on his nonsensical outcry; turning panic to joy, a foreword to our departure. It was morning, "Com-tee-ma-teh-la!", it was the hour we had awaited. Under this new beacon could we spot where to go, how to plan our next... day? Week? Month? Perhaps we wouldn't plan anything. We would simply be judged by the sun, before the evening should resurface.

30

Having communed, we sat in a circle. No crackers, no hummus, no granola bars, nothing to munch. Nothing to drink either. We were parched. We breathed – the only life-saving consumption left to us. It was a habit of ours to sit in a circle, not talking after concerts. We hadn't played a concert, but then maybe a concert was comparable a bond to what we had just loudly manifested. On second thought, the former had been much stronger. I was beyond drowsy, and could only think in the immediate. If my mind strayed, I entirely zoned out, and forgot where or what I was. My recollections are gelatinous, which must be noticeable. I cannot explain why the conversations that had preceded the dawn had been etched into my memory, to that extent I can recount them now (or, I am recounting something close to what I believe they had been). From the dawn on, howbeit, I cannot claim to such fidelity.

It's possible I slept a little in that circle, since from that moment on, I delineate clear images of The Rails. The countless flights of stairs, grey, used, slippery steps, dimly lit, down the seemingly bottomless staircase; and those occasions – the single, ancient elevator broken – when artists and techs had been constrained to lug amps, instruments, cables and pedal boards down those murky steps towards our chamber of euphoria. The wide staircase packed come opening time; the small square room at the final level, from which the main hall and the stage were visible. I always speculated the stairs were so poorly lit so that peoples' eyes would get used to the gloom, as The Rails was a place of perpetual obscurity (even the rudimentary stage lights, coloured spots were derelict, should have been renewed, most of them, two decades ago, though we liked it that way) – one would expect this from a literally underground rock club.

At that time I came to (out of sleep or fantasy), out of picturing The Rails – the glossy bomb-proof walls, the filthy ground, the ringing echoes – the others had discussed the idea I had thrown out in the air earlier. K. shook my shoulder, they were gazing at me, and questioned me: "So?" I asked what it was about, and they explained what I had missed. Either we left the instruments there, went out to see what was going on, and if possible, locate a generator in order to hold a concert. This plan entailed the risk of us not being able to come back to fetch our gear. Or, we put all our gear and ourselves into H.'s van, in the underground parking, however a tight fit it should prove, drive out, go to H.'s place, figure out the situation, and from there, have a concert where possible (here, maybe). The last options were to each grab our stuff and go our separate ways or, together, bolt for H.'s house, without any intent of a concert.

I had no idea what they wanted. I voted for "Well, H.'s van, then we come back here if we can?" Sim raised an eyebrow: "You really think we could drive out?" "What the fuck else we supposed to do? Wait for an invitation?" Ivan retorted.

31

A ridiculously tight fit. The van contained in addition to what it had brought in, K.'s two instruments, other equipment, two people... Loading, we had turned our heads at each resonating echoing rolls of common dings and rustle; dragging of shoes, or loud breathing... Unknowing if said noises were our own, or if we were being watched – from the walls oozed the eerie aura of eyes – and if empowered thugs could, at any moment, jump out, and we being on the wrong side of a riffle, would end up being taken hostage, or fed lead, then left for rat-feed; what knew we? Reality still augmented from previous peaks high for some; for others sick feelings in the pits of our growling entrails, growing migraines, photosensitive slit-eyed; we moved as a unit. While two brought equipment down, two in each location were guarding the gear. We were much more paranoiac in dead-silence than when hell had been breaking loose outdoors – go figure. To reach H.'s wheels, our huddle scuttled in the nearly-empty parking garage (there were a couple of abandoned vehicles), necks twisting, confusedly guarding our three-sixty.

And then came Tetris-packing our gear. Folding seats, lifting and shifting and replacing items. H. was driving, K. was sitting in the front passenger seat with a snare drum on her lap (the stand braced between her legs). Sim settled on Ivan's lap on the one remaining free seat. I was perched on an amp, with El. on my lap, uncertain if I should be feeling more or less guilt. But guilt for what? Most of the guilt in my veins flowed with a "too late now" diagnosis. My carcass was aching with that particular *down* from when the E fades, along with the other delicatessens. And my carcass was rejuvenated, a tight grasp around El.'s waist. My headache was surely motivation towards guilt – guilt towards myself, and towards everyone else. Why did I have to abuse my limits (the limits of my thankfully healthy body, as every body, with a potential for illness or collapse at any instant), and abuse my lady's limits – not El., but *my lady* –, two-timing her in her own insights? What was two-timing if it had been in her insights? I supposed it all laid exactly within my own pounding pulse and impulses, and how dearly I hated cherishing El. on my lap, or how easily I would betray blessed humdrum; shouldn't I? Was I a reflection of how the world was turning to shit? I had savoured a few affairs – not with this partner of mine (or had I...?) – but in previous relationships, and guilt had never been an issue for me. Because what was guilt in a one-night stand? Time spent with a stranger that would not lead any further – hello, goodbye, it was nice meeting you. El. was no stranger to-head-on-her-way. El. and I would meet again, longing would surge... or would it? These things can fade... And I'm unsure if any emotion can be adequately labeled – we were all of us exhausted, our cognitive skills depleted. And the sketch of a grin scarred my brooding; pushing our limits, hadn't it been an exercise in straining out the vileness, the worry, the dread of our rag-like anatomies: a survival mechanism? Auto-destructive survival; what a jerk I was excusing myself. Though what else were we supposed to do?

Cheating just as guilt was a conception I owed to my own judgment of what was right or wrong – not my partner; most probably my partner had been okay with it, she joking about it as she did, she joking about my *blushing* as she had. Because when El. and I had made love, it had felt like I would have rather been nowhere else; and that was the guilt. That it had felt right was the issue. Not empty sex that leaves indifferent, bad sex that leaves a bitterish aftertaste; rather it had been an alchemy from lead to gold shining, to forge an individual anew. It had felt right. And then, what may feel right – good – is not, at often times, compatible with what else may feel right – good, that is.

It creaked, in the van, as we advanced; the weight of our cargo could be felt in the engine's struggling tug.

Though I could excuse any *misbehavings* at that time, needed I excuse myself (to myself and-or everyone else) when H. was pulling out onto the street from the almost empty underground garage? An embarrassing gesture, an egotistical gesture when, on the opposite, humility, erasing self-regard while keeping a straight, standing-tall, face was necessary. No one thought or gave a damn about what I did or had done – we inhabited this tense moment in the objective of surviving it till the next. And I hadn't done anything to feel bad about – had I? –, I felt bad because of the *down*, depleted serotonin. Repeating within "Don't think about it. It's all bullshit. Fuck it, just keep going. Don't worry." It was not a time of fear, danger and neurosis, as it had been during the night (neurosis sedated, danger drugged).

Sim wanted to cower on the floor (as if it would have been safer), but couldn't, because there wasn't enough room. He was sitting on Ivan's lap, and Ivan was propping him up, complaining that Sim's cowering was crushing him, which it most probably did.

Things were rattling and shaking all over. H. was accelerating slowly, not knowing what to expect. Emerging out of the underground, the pallid avenues greeted us with a reassuring nil.

32

A few streets farther we were stopped by a roadblock. Featuring –
what a show – a tank! We had seen old models of these machines,
exhibited in parks, museums, or the likes. Non-functioning, closed, like
statues. We had never been in front of a functioning one, with its canon
moving, machine guns following our movements. H. brutally stomped
on the breaks when we were ordered to halt. The sight of so many
killing machines would certainly have brought her to halt even if no
megaphone had instructed her, us, to. The shock of the unexpected
breaking – however slowly we were rolling – unseated us, made one
drum topple over on another. I held El. yet more firmly for her not to
tumble and get hurt and so, I held her tightly against myself in this
moment of panic, of detestable panic, and her face close to mine, a
cheek against my cheek, her sweet jasmine aroma, my head turned as
did hers; she exhaled, and my lips touched her skin without kissing. I
pushed against the floor, braced my knees against the amp in front of it.
Tender was this parry to repel collapse, enclosing attentiveness on the
adjacent only essence to matter. To matter: if said goal targeted the
sum of our milieu, then let it motivate such claims as opposed to abutting
marvel. I wanted to show nothing but indifference at their tanks and
riffles, because they weren't for me. Instead, the whole of my ability
fell upon clinging to El. as hard as I could, as hard as she clung to me.
Had I taken dope, fear of death could have seemed funnier.

33

A prolonged wait. Time ticking in fact, or in impression, since easy it isn't to sit and refrain from movement for minutes on end. Then, orders, more orders, we all came out, showing our hands. The day was cooler than the night had been (as the previous day). We were ordered to stand here, ordered to stand there. I complained: we were just musicians, for crying out loud. The whole band begged me to shut up. I was ordered to shut up. They searched the van while we stood still and quiet. They searched us, interrogated H., deliberated with her. H. was more rested, she was our diplomat. We needed a diplomat. Not everyone could be their own diplomat. Not everyone would be listened to. Not everyone would make sense. Not everyone would be given the chance to make sense. To try and make sense. We had our diplomat, lucky for us.

Exactly at that time, I felt like I did want a new bass. True, I really did. Something changed within me? Or was it due to changes in the outside world, that I felt like I would need a new instrument? I think it was because in a time where weapons were turned towards me, I, in turn, needed my own weapon – however peaceful – to turn on others. Something to ward them off. I wanted to explore options with K.. If she were to construct it, I knew I could ask for anything. I would never want something as ridiculously complicated as her *Vanilla sound*, and I would absolutely not want her to name the instrument... but then, if the bass could have a piezo mode, with a very low, toneless, slightly muted sound, as to get a quasi up-right base tone. That would be nice for smoother tunes, or if ever we decided to delve into jazzier or bluesier material. I repeated this idea over and over again as to not forget it. Five times, ten times, sixteen, twenty-two, thirty-four, fifty-eight... I repeated this decision in my head while they were frisking me. I didn't feel their hands running up and down my legs, feeling my ribs, pulling down my trousers... I was thinking about a chambered bass with a piezo mode which would have the potential to sound like a double bass... Then I could session with "traditionalist" jazzmen, I would have the opportunity to attain thrilling opportunities, play more, diverse styles, meet new musicians, travel opportunities. I would... after we would go through the roadblock, go to H.'s place...

34

H., foot on the accelerator, told us she had gotten permission to drive us to her place where they had dictated we were to stay. Why would we have to? H. uttered; it wasn't so much a matter of choice as a matter of survival. "What should we survive, them? Others? All and the same?".

"Yea, well in any case, I have this laissez-passer to bring the lot of us to my place. That's that. Do whatever the hell you want, but I'm not negotiating anything else. Not like I'd have means to manage it. Dammit, you didn't hear what they said. Well, they didn't divulge much, mind you, they just said that a good few hundred people died last night. You hear that? Few hundred. That's a plural actually. Hundreds. Plural. You know..." H. rambled on.

I wished, then, that K. were in the back so that I could chat with her. I was visualizing what we could elaborate together – for that bass she had offered to make. Or she probably had many original body shapes in mind. She occasionally tried pushing wacky designs, crossing fingers for them not to fall flat as novelty gimmicks, but to be perceived as the beautiful result of imaginative craftsmanship.

I remember when she tried to market an acorn shaped guitar to a popular brand, but that thin, jangly, folk-rock sound oriented guitar did not catch on in the least, and I think she only made about 10 or 20, that took forever to sell. Mind you, 10-20 is a limited run, but still a good run in my opinion. As yet I can picture the head stock, carved like the crown of a tree, down to the details of carved-in leaf motives. Around the base of the neck, sprung the moulding of roots, and of course, the body was an acorn. Nice, simple, with two open coil mini-humbuckers, coil taps, deluxe. K. admitted that she wouldn't have grooved with it, but that she really had thought it would satisfy the many folk rock musicians around. After the poor initial run, she gave up the idea of producing a twelve-string version.

Of course K. never ran out of ideas, nevertheless my mind scanned the many models of basses in existence, other than those I owned, or had owned, or had tried but hadn't particularly dug. In my view, it would obviously have to be solid-body – what would be the point of changing, otherwise? One of the most tempting basses in pure aesthetics, for me, which wasn't "my sound" (as it was known for sustain, and harmonic texture – the opposite of my Hebros), was the great Gibson Thunderbird (the reverse body – let's be frank that the non-reverse was essentially the Fender offset shape). It had a smoothness to it, yet presence. It gave lots of neck access, though size was a downside for travel. It being a long-scale bass wasn't my preference – I dug the deeper oomph of short scale basses. The long neck, paired with the pickups in the middle and bridge positions gave the thunderbird a melodic inclination – in my opinion – which I never wanted, admitting that it was a good bass. The Jolana DiscoBass was similar, but more along the lines of what I sought (though a long scale also, the pickups were much fatter, or so I recall, having tried both Thunderbird and DiscoBass on rare occasions, never comparing them side by side). I could fool myself that I just wanted a DiscoBass; but the point of switching basses was K.'s ability to deliver a better and unique instrument. As much as there is an objective *better* apart from *different*. Plus, a DiscoBass... "Good luck getting your hands on one now", I told myself. Their short production run in the late 1980's left too few of them in the world. Another interesting, and drastically different choice in style would be the diamond shaped Jolana Star IX bass – a body shape K. adored; having to chose from the blue and the orange options, blue would keep me more discrete... but when change is needed, why not go with the flashy orange? I had tried a Star IX during our first album tour, when we opened for the more successful band *Opioid tarantula*. One of their two bass players had a modified version (the pickups had already been changed when she had acquired it, she claimed). Then again, as long as change happened, at that pace, I could end up with a Warlock or Dragon Wing shaped bass. Perhaps we could learn towards more purposeful body shapes, like an L-bow, or an Imperial (the Imperial's long shoulder could reach higher too – when did I ever wrap my hand around the neck?). I could always gravitate towards classics though, never having played on an SG shape... And so, the fantasy of a Hagström h8 resurfaced. When I pondered the potential of "the new", I, as a rule, am sent back to the astoundingness of what already exists.

I was overwhelmed with lust for each of these interesting and radically different body shapes. All I knew is that I wanted a slightly narrower yet thicker neck than the standard was – that was the neck of my Hebros, and I liked that kind of a neck. What would be my other desired specifications? I had never thought about getting a custom-made instrument because I had always personally thought them to be superfluous. A little like Ivan, though with a diverging outlook. I found the least gear to get the job done, the better. That if you need loads of gear to sound good, then you're bad... but, not always, in regards to the nature of the final product. Ready to brawl with any disciples of the idea that eye-for-detail and super-expensive gear meant better sound, I needed only to state the fact that most of the greatest rock-and-roll out there had been made with old, or cheaper instruments; that few of the truly great artists could afford high-end or custom instruments until they had become known, and had perhaps (usually) produced their best material (some if not most of it). Disregarding that a number of high-quality instruments, unpopular, had become cheap, only to see their prices soar once rediscovered, like Wandre instruments had – price meant next to nothing. The strongest, most innovative sounds, came from the equipment artists could afford, and what they could afford was at best "top factory made". Would we have to detail how former budget brands like Silvertone and Harmony became so sought-after decades later? How gold-foil Teisco and DeArmond pickups came into fashion at a time when people understood that though they were cheap to produce, no other pickups had the same genial sound. And then there was a time when makers launched their own versions of back-in-popularity gold-foils. Cost had been mistaken for quality, and as per usual, low cost with low quality. Such fallacious logic can fool our brains but not our ears. Trained and untrained ears might not appreciate things in the same way, but they hear nonetheless, and the feelings created by "cheap" sounds have no fewer charms... Granted, some people might be snob enough to suppress their appreciation of "cheap sounds", even if their bodies may move to the groove and minds clasp particular harmony. I had never considered having an instrument made to my specific wishes, details, whims, not only for price reasons, but perhaps because I thought that there were so many good or interesting instruments in the world already. Why would I want to make one more, when so many poor orphans needed a home? A few times, I had even, when they appeared along my path, collected broken or badly beaten instruments, and brought them to K. for her to fix (and sell, afterwards). Though that hadn't happened for a spell. The last I recalled, was before I found my Hebros. I had stumbled on another old Bulgarian instruments. One elderly dude had, in his shed, an Orfeus Trimontium. I could only recognize it by its greyed hook-like headstock. The finish had entirely peeled off, the body looked like it had been dragged behind a car. Only fortunately had the wood veneer not cracked. I felt so sad for the old Trimontium. It reeked of death, I felt like it shouldn't be touched, like it bore a self-mumbled curse, exuding hatred unto those who had deformed and mutilated its hulk, then left it in the murk. Yet, my duty was that of taking it in an attempt at restoration. The old man, who had not known what to do with it for the latter part of his life, gave it to me for free. In the end K. succeeded in saving it, and sold it to a happy greenhorn. There were so many instruments out there, so many good instruments; why would I have wanted something made only for me?

K. had offered said gift, though, and at this time I felt like it was what I needed. To ward the rest of them off. Defend myself against this onslaught of insanity. A weapon in my own image, to my liking. A weapon not to destroy life, but to make it meaningful – a thing some might find more dangerous. Or rather, not a weapon, let us forget weapons of any sort; rather a self-portrait to save oneself from moot time.

—   Are you okay? Asked El.

—   Oh yea, I'm fine, I was just thinking about what K. offered me yesterday.

—   What was that, queried K. turning around in her seat.

—   That bass you offered to make for me. I was thinking of different body shapes, but then again, we'll look at that together. Short scale, narrow frets, narrower but thicker neck... and I liked that *mudbucker* you mentioned, that at the neck, like an old EB, or to get that low Rivoli rumble...

—   Yea well... looks like that'll have to wait, she affirmed, jaw tightened by frustrated angst.

—   How come?

—   Jeez man, haven't you heard what they just announced on the radio?

—   No, I'm sorry, I was daydreaming.

The van overtaken by silence of the most mundane. I gazed at El., but she just stared through the side window we faced. I looked at Sim and Ivan, and their heads were veered towards the front of the van. I noticed we were slowing down. I tried to side-glance to the windshield, and spotted jarheads on both sides of the road.

34

I was stunned by H.'s attack. She yelled "Don't you ever just deal with sorrow, without trying to elude it?" I was pondering aloud, "why the fuck would I want to be sad, and keep on being sad?" That seemed obvious, no? Why shouldn't someone try to avoid sadness, and instead, linger on such dread feelings? "Well, whatever's going on, can't we talk anymore?" I countered. She didn't reply. It was already mid-afternoon, and we were only now coming to the house where she lived. It had taken us the whole day to get through the numerous blockades. Fortunately, at one of them, Ivan had hatched the idea of pleading to the butchers, crying we hadn't had anything to eat or drink since the night before, when we had remained locked in an empty building to avoid the exterior conflicts. The military man still had a human side to him, and was able to provide us with a couple of small boxes of "rations", and bottles of water. "I'm not hungry now, my stomach is like a knot" H., behind the wheel, requested we keep hers for the time of our arrival. At that point El. asked me "Do you know any way you can get in contact with your girlfriend? They said they shut down all the lines", so I pointed out "obviously, I don't." And the answer left me in pure panic. What did I have in this world?

I opened a packet of biscuits, the last of my rations. I had kept it to munch on before we would get to our new abode. H.'s abode. Our meanwhile abode. Indefinite meanwhile. I had a hard time telling how fast the sun was setting, given that I didn't have a good view out the windshield, and the side windows were tinted. I didn't want to upset H. more than she already was, so I begged El., Sim and Ivan in a low voice, if they couldn't liven up the mood a little. Ivan frowned at me "You can ask that, man, you've got clothes in your case, and a backpack. I don't have a change of underwear. My balls are sweaty, man." I replied "Hey, don't worry, you and anyone else can borrow some of mine. It wouldn't be the first time. Or some of H.'s panties. She probably wouldn't mind; I bet it wouldn't be the first time you wore panties either." But he shook his head "Sorry, it's not just the underwear. I guess I was just brushing things off for so long too." "So why stop now?" I laughed. That did get him to smile. He shrugged his shoulders, looked Sim in the face, Sim shrugged his shoulders. I looked at El., and she softly sighed "suppose we'd have to try to know what to do for real."

We agreed with her. Whatever it meant, what she said. We all agreed with her, though there wasn't so much we could do. Any plans we could make at this time were vague, nothing could be known long term. Except for what we wanted, in the long run. Only our desires could be known. (So shouldn't only they count?) That was the only thing in the world that we could control – what we, as individuals, desired, eventually, when we could get it, if ever we could get it. Wasn't that what our whole lives had been? Our band? Weren't we working abusively hard, long hours, non-paying work, in the hopes that perhaps one day, we could really live only from our passions (though K. would always make and repair instruments, for her own pleasure, I was guessing)? No one in the world could calculate a musician's hourly wage if you counted practice time – it would look too sad. Even famous musicians, if you count the ten-hour practice sessions from their early days, their "famous" wages would drop massively in equalization pay. Whatever wealth they had, they had acquired through years of bottom-feeding, and being screwed over by accepting any gig, any poorly paying gig, if paying (and not remunerated through glorious *exposure*), in order to become known, to have their names out there, in order to perhaps start earning money from their work. And that had been our lives, to some good extent. We had only not so long ago become *established*, by reputation that is, and to a reasonable extent, *in demand* (albeit not enough to avoid feeling the pinch). I whispered "What hasn't been real?", but no one answered.

I thought, onraging occurrences were no different from anything else we had experienced in life (and yes, *in life*, because we may experience in dream, or imagination, or by association, or empathy), it was just more intense. And harder times to come, if people would be too stubborn to make peace – would rather kill off more of their kin –, we would experience starvation, and pain, wounds perhaps, disease, sorrow, to extents we had never known, we would not imagine? Or had we? It wasn't the degree of barbarity of a circumstance that would affect one the most, but the shock it brought about.

While discussing this, Ivan recalled, in childhood, meeting a political refugee his parents had housed until he could secure lodgings his own. Every night, that man would take medication in order to have no dreams, and more medication to still the anxiety and anguish stemming from trauma. Indiscreet as some children are, Ivan had probed about his story. And confessed the man, amidst the years of imprisonment and torture, the unhealable wound that radiated hurt, was not said persecution, but his son's passing. A child of three, infected with an illness to cut him down before the age of four. Though curable, their country offered only private healthcare: not even mafias legal or clandestine could enable them to secure the funds necessary to save his son's life, through domestic or abroad treatments accessible. Ordinary folk who had toiled for average wages; they had savings, but not enough, and no "collateral" to borrow by. Day after day, he would seek out help, contact relatives, ask neighbours, and watch his son die. Day after day he would cry in panic. Trying his hardest, unable to prevent his loved one from reaching a feverish tomb. Those were his nightmares – pacing, yelling at strangers "my whole world will die! Won't you help?", standing in front of clinics, pleading politicians, meeting other powerless parents, relatives... His nightmares took place in living rooms, at his son's bedside. He saw his little one in pain, weeping. He heard the child's loud cries echoing in the apartment, incessantly, for hours. He saw scenes that were *completely banal*, unfolded in plain sights, settings.

The prison? The torture? They could deliver no anguish greater than that he knew. He had told young Ivan he was already dead. He had no feelings, and refused upon himself rightful suicide only for one thing: getting back at his country, destroying as much as possible. When he had met parents and relatives, or sick people, sick people who could have been saved, he noticed there were numerous, and yet, they were powerless when they only begged. Begging wasn't enough; they had to demand. So, he joined a terrorist front. He could die, death was nothing. His wife had passed, clear of conscience, throwing herself with a bomb on a politician ex-banker's car. He said he didn't want to do the same, only to blow up more than one car. He wanted to assassinate more than one culprit. He wanted to assassinate the lot of them. His lapse in this, asylum ours, was no respite – only time to reroute. Ivan recounted this.

He nodded "pain can come from anywhere, at any time. There is no criteria for feeling pain. That man, he's dead now. I can't forget him. He said that pain was being powerless. That the worst feeling you could ever imagine, was being entirely powerless. Incapable of anything. In front of you, distress, injustices, in front of you crimes, in front of you, things so terrible you could in no way have foreseen them, you cannot change the despicable status quo; your might as a single conscious soul has reached its limits, and you realize that other factors in the world work against you. That is true pain. Pain is being powerless. That's what he said. It's all about what one is prepared for. Trauma comes from your singular experience. Like physical trauma, physical wounds, it is not a specific fall that would hurt you, but the way in which you fall. Though, of course... some falls would kill anyone".

Sim came into the conversation, voice crackling "yea, but none of us have felt that sort of pain before, no? I haven't. I have never felt like I wanted to die, like I was so afraid. None of us have, right? I hope none of us will." And he sighed a long pause before adding "I was thinking about joining the defence force." We gawked at him wide-eyed. I was speechless. Ivan challenged "Why would you do that?", and Sim explained "Should I die hiding in a basement, or should I die standing up for myself." K. let slip "for yourself, or for them?" Sim always did have a brash, rash behaviour (chugging *the sludge*); some of what gave him that stage energy and charisma. "So you're thinking of becoming part of the very thing you're afraid of, because it's less scary to be part of a problem than to let it run its course, run about, around us, without knowing what it's up to", rambled I, but he interrupted me. "Maybe it's not a problem... I mean, maybe it's our problem, I mean..." I listlessly frowned at him "Bottom line is, you want to take part in something which you're against." He got frustrated "you know you really are an asshole?". Ivan looked at me too and shrugged once more, a jauntily distant grin adorned, *admitted* "you can be a dick sometimes." El. turned around and kissed me; "Everyone always loses when they don't compromise." Ivan rattled on "Think about when we jam, man. You want to play one thing, maybe the other musicians don't get into it, they can't play on top of what you're playing. Maybe it's too complex, maybe it's just not the right mood. They ad lib, you have to listen to them, they have to listen to you. You follow them, they follow you, that's how it goes." I muttered "nobody jams with a gun." Ivan stared at Sim "don't go joining no defence forces."

35

We pulled into the driveway at H.'s house. Woozy from the ride and the lack of air – even with windows opened – and the whiffs of strange fumes seeping through the open windows now and again, relief submerged us more as a memory than actual solace.

The whole district showed row after row of beautiful brick or wooden houses, with lace-like sculpted decorations under the slanted roofs or around windows, and cone-shaped gables. Deserted streets: we hadn't seen anyone since the last checkpoint.

36

We had carried our equipment inside without exchanging a single word. Late afternoon, the air had cooled; after the stuffy sauna of the van, it felt at once both chilly and soothing, dense in evanescent seasonal aromas.

H. had tossed me the keys to lock up. I galumphed out of the kitchen – with its linoleum flooring, it was the first room when entering the house – to return to the van, trying my best to see through the opaque penumbra flooding each corner, my pupils weary. The adamant firmament lightened my mood; cities deprived of their polluting bulbs gifted us with the cosmos. For that, I was pleased.

I checked that we had left nothing in the entire sweat-reeking vehicle, half-blinded by the dull glow of the ceiling lamp, before heading back, and in heading back, El. and I bumped into one another. Not knowing there was nothing left to be hauled, and that I was locking the van, she had come back to help some more. Grateful to be outdoors and stretch our legs, this evening ultimately, after the whole day, six of us in the snail-paced wagon, we chattered, hung around, breathed in the untroubled breeze.

"We're not supposed to stay outside." "I know." But we weren't out for a stroll in the middle of central avenue, we were directly beside our shelter, we could have been out for a smoke. El. laughed "I'd enjoy a smoke", but my weed leftovers were inside. We didn't head inside though. Not at once. She leaned against the side of the garage (we were in a narrow passage between the house and the garage), and earnestly asked if really I wasn't afraid. "I try not more than at any other time", I chuckled, "They've been hanging this situation over our noodles for the last two or so years. It hasn't killed us yet." "It might though" she blushed, and I replied "so might anything else." She whispered "It's happening for real now", before I kissed her, and she kissed me back. "Yes it is"; we pulled each other in more closely. She knew I was as afraid as everyone else.

When that brief interlude had run its course, and the dusk-warning air felt too cold, we went back inside where the musky redolence of grass hit our nostrils. The band was seated in the kitchen, drinking beer. The bottles were so chilled that drops of condensation were running down their elongate brown necks. What was going on? They said they had counted our perishable and non-perishable foods, were concerned about how little we had, sat clueless, wondering where or how we could get more. "At the store, no?" I suggested. And they glared at me: "stores are closed."

Maybe that can be the fee for our concert, out in the garage, tomorrow or the day after, I hinted.

– Hey, man, the garage might... H. stammered; no one can go out, it's over! Just read a book, hibernate, wait for it to blow over. That's all we can do.

– I think we could still do it, mumbled K. with a flicker of a smile, puffing on reefer.

– Someone's on my side! I yipped.

– I mean, since we're waiting for it to be over anyway, why not busy ourselves on the down-low? Sim thinks we're going to die, might as well die playing music, reckoned Ivan.

El. asked for a brew. I asked for a brew. We sat down with everyone else. The lights were off. The lights were off in all houses. We had been instructed – a new law of sorts – no lights could be on when it would be dark out (on... noticeable; low lighting with blinds closed... might pass). It wasn't dark out yet, but it was getting there. Loose lace day curtains hung off the sides of our porthole frame, an amethyst skyline trampled by soiled clouds, a landscape denied to we aliens of our own lands beyond.

Ivan asked how we would get word around if we were to organize a concert. "The only ways left; door to door, word of mouth. Slip notes under doors in the dead of night. You think they will monitor every square inch round the clock? No way they're going to check every street at four AM."

"No way", ambiguously (dis)agree Sim.

37

Anew engulfed in a dusk locked away, just the six of us, quarantined mad, or quarantined from madness, angelic in vacuous, cynical, optimism. We had pulled arguments for and against clandestine gigging – one gig, for the least –, had been through all sorts of scenarios (scenarios in which we did arrange one, and scenarios in which we didn't; since it was necessary to take into account the risks of not partaking in resistance of our own brand, mad or against madness, and some of those scenarios were more dangerous than the ones in which we did organize a show – an imbecile fully trusts the benefits of sitting inactive, confused, on one's backside). H. wasn't so much against a gathering, as against the noise and the light it would cause – and her owning the premises did give her authority in the matter, which no one else could claim.

The outdoors were quiet, with only trees rustling to prove to us that life had not ceased. I had zoned out, kissed El., – or K.'s friend, or Elvira, or however I were to call her after these strange times. I had had enough blabbering spiralling around those heads of ours, banded together determined not to succumb to so satisfying much needed sleep, and I wanted us to come to a decision. Something resembling a decision; a conclusion, a milestone, our own kind of checkpoint. Without some decision, what was I to do with myself? I had no idea what to hope for if we didn't pursue our singularity, or to say, our band, the purpose it gave. I stepped up, hoping to state what had to be stated.

– So what do we do? It might all go down tonight. All these houses might burn, we might never walk freely again. We might have to follow rank-and-file. "Our" guys might force us to, other guys might force us to, they're all the same. Sim, you wanted to fight? But what's fighting? What are you fighting for, and what are you fighting with? I know you've all been looking at me like a naysayer, like a pain because I don't want to "welcome" these events recent or remote. I don't read the news, I don't watch the news, I don't talk about news, and politics, and the world with people – I stopped doing that a long while ago, and never picked it up again. They were shocked, in the train I rode over here. They were whispering here and there, in that smelly, humid wagon, 'bout how they were terrified 'bout taking the train, hearing rumours that some tracks might be booby-trapped, how the train might derail... And they didn't get it when I asked them to leave me alone. Because I didn't care... I didn't want to care. I accept whatever goes on, as long as I can do what I want. That is, as long as I feel free. Sufficiently free. As long as I am left alone to do my thing. You're all judging me in your own ways because I reject the dictatorial pressure of others to conform, and act the same, and share gossip. Fine! I want to do something, the same I've always done. I will fight, whoever, on my own terms. And the way I want to fight will be with my instrument, with our words, our work. We will fight with our accomplishments. We will fight with our songs that others may sing to attain their own personal victories. I will fight, you hear me? And this is how I want to fight. I want to mock those who shut us in here, and who tell us we can't go for a damn walk outside, not much differently than how they shut us in all of our lives, even when we could take damn walks outside, and who tell us we have to recoil into obscurity. I'll fight them, whoever they are, you get that? It's not that late. Autumn is lovely; a stage transitional, a stage in itself, everything transitional. It's dark out, but it's not very late. It's still the evening – dark but not night yet. The evening is upon us, not night yet, and we are as confused as when we arose, sleep deprived, after what I will remember as a wonderful vigil. Not the night it should have been, in front of a lively crowd of our kind – the kind of people for whom the world has a higher purpose, an artistic purpose, who fight with music instead of bloodshed, or aggression – at The Rails, deep underground, a converted remnant of former paranoia... the same paranoia we are going through now... the very same... We would have celebrated with champagne, backstage, with friends in our shelter... it wasn't that evening, where our art would have triumphed in that old bunker, a place repurposed because at one time, we thought we wouldn't need its likes anymore... I will remember our night as beautiful, though. The rounded-top window, biggest I've ever seen up close, the Art Deco interior, our trips, being close to each and everyone one of you, like we are close when we travel... When we stood up from that beautiful night, tired, cranky, confused, we were no better off than we are now – except for the food. The evening is upon us, not night yet; do you think all our can should cease here? I do not. I don't expect to lie down as time kills us; am I the only one of us who is not robbed of his interest in this world? Or am I? Have I been? I don't know what to do if we don't act... perform. If you chose we shouldn't, if you chose we abandon ourselves, then tell me what we're supposed to do.

9 789363 545472